PUFFIN CLASSICS

Tales of the Greek Heroes

In the house of Epimetheus stood a golden box which Prometheus had left there with strict orders that no one was to open it. Epimetheus told his wife this, but she was so curious and inquisitive that life did not seem worth living until she knew what treasure it was that her husband was hiding from her.

So one day when he was out, Pandora crept quietly to the golden casket and lifted the lid. Then with a rush and a cry out came all the ills which beset mankind – diseases, and sorrows, hate, jealousy, lies, theft, cheating, and a hundred others.

ROGER LANCELYN GREEN

Tales of the Greek Heroes

INTRODUCED BY
RICK RIORDAN

Illustrations by ALAN LANGFORD

PUFFIN CLASSICS

PUFFIN BOOKS

UK | USA | Canada | Ireland | Australia
India | New Zealand | South Africa

Puffin Books is part of the Penguin Random House group of companies
whose addresses can be found at global.penguinrandomhouse.com.

puffinbooks.com

First published 1958
First published in Puffin Books 1994
Reissued in this edition 2015

002

Text copyright © Roger Lancelyn Green, 1958
Illustrations copyright © Alan Langford, 1994
Introduction copyright © Rick Riordan, 2009
Endnotes copyright © Penguin Books, 2009

Set in Minion by Palimpsest Book Production Limited, Falkirk, Stirlingshire
Printed in Great Britain by Clays Ltd, St Ives plc

A CIP catalogue record for this book is available from the British Library

ISBN: 978–0–141–32528–6

www.greenpenguin.co.uk

INTRODUCTION BY
RICK RIORDAN

Before Luke Skywalker, before Batman, before even King Arthur, there were the Greek heroes. Those guys knew how to fight!

Imagine being trapped in a dark maze with no weapons, facing a three-metre-tall mutant with the head of a bull. Imagine being forced to do twelve jobs for your worst enemy: little things like stealing the Lord of the Dead's guard dog, slaying an eight-headed hydra or cleaning 12 billion kilos of manure out of a stable. Imagine facing an enemy like Medusa, who could turn you to stone with a single glance.

When I was a kid, I wanted to be a Greek hero. I wished I could face their challenges. Well, okay, maybe not the stable-cleaning task, but everything else sounded pretty cool. I wanted to borrow Perseus's sword, mirrored shield and winged shoes. I wanted to sail on the *Argo* with Jason to find the Golden Fleece. I wanted to be as strong as Hercules and pulverize giants with my bare fists.

This book, by Roger Lancelyn Green, was one of my

first introductions to the amazing world of Greek mythology. If it weren't for this book, I probably never would have written my own books about a modern-day demigod, Percy Jackson. If you like fantasy, comics, action and adventure movies, horror or any other type of story with heroes and monsters, you will love *Tales of the Greek Heroes*, because Greek mythology is where it all started.

In this collection you will face fire-breathing bulls and many-headed dragons. You will meet clever sorceresses, treacherous centaurs, jealous gods and evil kings. You will sail into unknown waters, soar up to Mount Olympus and descend into Hades. Not every story will have a happy ending, because a hero's journey is never easy and often fatal, but along the way you will meet many loyal friends and courageous allies.

Ready to get started? Fasten your armour. Grab your shield. Make sure your sword is sharpened. Within these pages are monsters that have been waiting 3,000 years to fight you. It's time you showed them who's boss.

Dedicated to the memory of
Emily and Gordon Bottomley

Once we fared with the *Argo*, sailing
The ancient seas for the Fleece of Gold,
The distant gleam and the song prevailing
Over the dragon guards of old;

And we have wandered the Islands ringing
With the Aegean thunder still,
Plucked the unfaded blossoms springing
Yet for us on the Muses' hill

After Euripides
Hypsipyle

Contents

CHAPTER ONE

The Coming of the Immortals

What forms are these coming
So white through the gloom?
What garments out-glistening
The gold-flower'd broom?

First hymn they the Father
Of all things; and then
The rest of Immortals,
The action of Men.

MATTHEW ARNOLD
Empedocles on Etna

1

If ever you are lucky enough to visit the beautiful land of Greece you will find a country haunted by more than three thousand years of history and legend.

The towering mountains slope steeply into the bluest of blue seas, and between the mountains lie valleys green and silver with the leaves of a million olive trees; golden with corn in the early summer, and then brown and white as the hot sun dries all up until the wide rivers become tinkling streams wandering in great courses of grey and yellow stones.

In winter and early spring the mountains are clothed

with snow; mist hides the higher lands, and the rivers are roaring torrents racing down into the great gulfs and bays which break up Greece into little divisions as surely as the mighty mountains do.

As you wander through Greece in the late spring you are back in those ancient days the moment you leave the towns behind. Up on the green slopes below the towering heights of the great mountains, of Parnassus or Taygetus or Cithaeron, you can sit and dream yourself back into the time when you might expect to meet an Immortal on the mountain, in the olive-groves, or in the lonely valleys.

Far away a shepherd pipes to his flock, magic notes stealing up through the warm silence: surely that is Pan, half-goat, half-human, who guarded the shepherds of old?

Among the olive leaves stand the broken columns of temples, grey, or white, or golden-yellow: every one has a tale to tell – a legend, a story, or an actual history.

Over the blue sea, with its streaks like purple wine, lie islands dotted away into the distance: and they too have each a tale to tell. It may be Delos, perhaps: no one lives on it now, but the ruins of cities and temples, harbours and theatres, cluster from the shore to the hilltop on which Apollo the Shining One and his sister Artemis the Maiden Huntress were born. Or it may be rocky, rugged Ithaca, from which Odysseus sailed to the siege of Troy, and found again after ten years' wandering over strange and dragon-haunted seas.

With all the breath-taking beauty of Greece round about them, it is hardly wonderful that the ancient Greeks felt that the mountains and the valleys, the woods and streams, the very sea itself, were peopled with Immortals. There were wood-nymphs among the trees and water-nymphs in the rivers – fairies of human size who did not die and had powers which mortals do not possess. There were sea-nymphs too – mermaids, though not all of them had tails – and strange sea-beings, who might be cruel and fierce even as the sea was fierce and cruel when the storms arose. And the sea must have a King, more powerful even than the nymphs, the Immortal called Poseidon who might come up through the waters in his chariot drawn by white horses, waving his trident – the three-pronged spear which was his sceptre, or sign of power.

On land also there were Immortal powers. Apollo, shining like the sun, who was also the lord of music and poetry; Artemis the Huntress who guarded all wild things; fierce Ares the warlord, whose terrible shout might ring across the field of battle when the spears were flying and the swords of bronze or iron clanged on the shields and helmets; Athena, Immortal Lady of wisdom; the kind Mother Goddess, Demeter, who caused the corn to grow and the young lambs to be born, with her lovely daughter Persephone who had to spend half the year in the kingdom of the dead when dark winter was spread over the earth.

Then there was Aphrodite, Immortal Lady of Beauty and Love, with Eros her son who shot the invisible arrows that made a young man or girl fall in love; there was Hephaestus, more skilled than any mortal man in working with bronze and gold and iron, whose forge was beneath the island of Lemnos, with a volcano as his furnace-chimney; there was Hermes of the winged heels, swift messenger, more cunning than any human; there was Dionysus who gave such power to the grapes that they could be brewed into wine to be a joy and a comfort to mankind; and there was the quiet Hestia, Lady of the home and guardian of the hearth – for the hearth was the heart of the home in the days when fire was difficult to make.

All these, and more, were the Immortals, and their powers were great. But they too must surely obey laws and have a ruler set over them – and this was Zeus, the King of Heaven and of Earth, who wielded the thunder-bolt, and was father of Mortals and of Immortals; and his Queen was Hera, Lady of Marriage and guardian of children. Zeus had power over all Immortals, though he seldom exercised it over his brothers, Poseidon, Lord of the Sea, and Hades, Lord of the Dead, whose kingdom of shadows was thought to be beneath the earth.

The Greeks called these Immortals the 'Gods', and worshipped them, making sacrifices to them at their particular shrines: Zeus at Olympia, Apollo at Delphi, Athena at Athens, and so on. When they began to tell the stories about them they had very little idea of what gods should be, and quite naturally pictured them as very like themselves, but much more powerful, more beautiful, and more free. Nor did it seem wrong to them to imagine that gods and goddesses could be cruel, or mean, deceitful, selfish, jealous, or even wicked, according to our ideas, and as they themselves would have thought if ordinary men and women had done as the gods did.

Another trouble was that the Greeks in each of the little kingdoms and cities, and in the islands, made up different stories more or less without knowing what was being told over the sea, or beyond the mountains. Then, later, when minstrels travelled from place to place, and writing became more common, and people began to meet those from other parts of the Greek world, they found that many of the stories did not agree.

'Hera is the wife of Zeus,' the people of Argolis would say. 'Nonsense!' the Arcadians would answer. 'He married Maia, and they had a son called Hermes!' 'What are you talking about?' the people of Delphi or Delos would protest: 'The wife of Zeus is called Leto, and they had two children called Apollo and Artemis!'

Well, there was only one thing for it: they had to agree that Zeus must have had several wives! But Hera, as the most important of the Immortals, was obviously the real

Queen of Heaven – and, as a woman would be, she was jealous!

In the earliest days the Greeks themselves often had several wives, as the people of Egypt did, and as the Turks and the Indians did until quite recently. In Greece, however, there was usually one real wife, and the others were captives taken in war, who were treated more and more as mere slaves; well looked after, but obliged to do just as they were told.

So it was not difficult to think of Zeus or Apollo behaving in much the same way as such a King of Athens as Theseus: and of course, over in Asia, kings always had many wives. That was where Troy was, so naturally King Priam had fifty sons, and Hecuba, the Queen of Troy, was simply his chief wife.

Each of the little Greek kingdoms, or city-states, had its own Royal Family; and each Royal Family liked to trace its descent back to one of the gods. It was much the same in England a thousand years ago: Alfred the Great was said to be descended from Odin, who held just the same place among the Saxons and the Danes as Zeus did among the Greeks. Indeed, if we believe the old writers of the Middle Ages, our own Royal Family, right down to the present Queen herself, can trace its descent from Odin on the one hand, and from Antenor who was the cousin of Priam of Troy, on the other!

Certainly Hera had some reason to be jealous – and she

was very jealous indeed, or so the stories tell us – of Zeus's mortal wives: and he had one in nearly every kingdom, just as sailors were said to have a wife in every port!

When the Greeks began to tell stories of the gods and goddesses, they had not become very civilized, so the legends seemed quite normal and credible to them. But as time went on, and the Greeks thought and learned more and more, some at least of them began to wonder about many of the stories: they began to realize that there was only one real God, and that he was good – better than any man could be.

Surely, however, this God must be Zeus: therefore Zeus himself must have become better and better, and have learnt by suffering until he understood what Mercy really meant.

Then the story-tellers realized that this fitted in rather well with the oldest of the stories about the gods. For in the very early days, before Zeus came, there were other gods – terrible creatures who were hardly people at all – who were as cruel and as dreadful as a tempest or an earthquake, as a tidal wave or an erupting volcano. These, in the earliest stories of all, those made by savage ancestors ages before, were the children of the Sky and the Earth. They were Giants and Titans, terrible ogres and trolls with many hands, or snake-like tails; and the most terrible of them was called Cronos – and he was the father of the real gods, of Zeus, Poseidon, Hades, and of the goddesses Hera, Hestia, and Demeter.

We need not try to imagine what Cronos was like. The Greeks who invented the stories about him cannot have done so. His name means Time – but it was only the Romans who began to picture him as kindly old Father Time, with his scythe and his hourglass.

The original Cronos was horribly different. He had a scythe, indeed, or rather a sickle – but he used it to cut pieces off his father Uranus, or Sky!

'You may be our ruler now!' Sky told him. 'But your children will treat you just as you have treated us and worse. They will bind you in a terrible prison, and one of them will rule instead of you!' And what Sky said, Earth said also, and Cronos knew that Earth cannot tell lies.

'We'll see about that!' roared Cronos, and he began to swallow his children as soon as they were born – just as Time swallows up the years, one after another.

First he swallowed Hestia, and then Demeter and Hera, and after them Hades and Poseidon.

This was too much for his wife, Rhea, although she was much the same kind of creature as Cronos; and as soon as her youngest son, Zeus, was born, she hid him away in a cave on the island of Crete.

'Where is the child?' demanded savage Cronos, and Rhea gave him a great stone wrapped in baby-clothes – and he swallowed that, thinking it was Zeus.

But Zeus was safe enough in Crete, guarded by the mountain-nymphs, the children of kindly Mother Earth.

When he was fully grown, Zeus sought counsel of the good Titaness Metis, or Thought, who gave him a magic herb which he put into Cronos's wine. It made Cronos very sick, and up came the swallowed children, still very much alive, and all very angry.

The stone came up too, and you may see it to this very day just where it fell, at Delphi. Beside it is another stone which Zeus placed there to mark the centre of the earth: for he let loose two eagles, one from either end of the world, and they met exactly over Delphi.

Then for ten years Zeus, with his brothers and sisters, fought against Cronos and the Titans, and at last beat them, with the aid of the Cyclopes. These were giants with only one eye each, which was in the middle of the forehead. They made thunderbolts which Zeus showered down on his foes; and they made the trident with which Poseidon stirred up the sea to drown his enemies; and they made a helmet of invisibility for Hades, who, when he wore it, could creep up unseen behind the Titans.

When the war was ended, Zeus shut up Cronos and the Titans in a fiery prison under the earth called Tartarus; and in after days the souls of the wicked were sent there to suffer with them.

Zeus and his brothers then cast lots to see which should rule the air, which the sea, and which under the earth:

and so Zeus became the King of Heaven, Poseidon ruled the waves, and Hades the realm of the dead.

Then there was peace, and Zeus caused the palaces of the gods to be built: but whether their golden home was on Mount Olympus in the north of Greece, or on some cloud-mountain high up in the heavens, the Greeks were not quite certain.

After this Zeus began to restore the bruised and battered earth, for the Titans had thrown great mountains about, and brought desolation wherever they went.

Not all the Titans had taken part in the war, for the stories say that Helios, who drove the chariot of the Sun, was a Titan, and so was Selene, the Moon, and so too was Ocean, the very sea itself. And there were Metis, or Thought, Themis, or Justice, and Mnemosyne, or Memory, the mother of the Nine Muses, who lived on Mount Helicon. The Muses, of course, attended to the Arts – History, Lyric Poetry, Comedy, Tragedy, Dancing, Love-Poetry, Hymns, Epic, and Astronomy; and they were the special companions of Apollo.

One of the Titans who were imprisoned in Tartarus was Iapetus. He had three sons, two of whom helped Zeus in many ways. The third son, the only one who *looked* like a Titan, was Atlas; who fought against Zeus, and for a punishment was made to stand on top of Mount Atlas in North Africa and hold up the sky on his shoulders.

The two helpful sons of Iapetus were Prometheus and Epimetheus; and the first of these was one of the most important figures in all Greek myth.

CHAPTER TWO

HERMES AND APOLLO

There through the dews beside me
  Behold a youth that trod,
With feathered cap on forehead,
  And poised a golden rod.

With lips that brim with laughter
  But never once respond,
And feet that fly on feathers,
  And serpent-circled wand.

A. E. HOUSMAN
The Merry Guide

2

Before the great war with the Titans there had been men on the earth, and that time was the Golden Age when the corn grew without ploughing or sowing, and all the animals lived on fruit or grass.

The Golden Age came and passed, for no children were born, and the men and women did nothing but eat and drink, and wander about the lovely garden of the world.

Then came the men of the Silver Age, and with them came wickedness and evil, because of Cronos and the Titans; and they were destroyed utterly from the earth and were imprisoned with their wicked makers in Tartarus.

But when Zeus sat throned in Olympus, and the great war was over, he called to him the good Titan Prometheus.

'Go,' he said, 'and make Man out of clay. Make him in shape and form like the Immortals, and I will breathe life into him. Then you shall teach him such things as he needs to know, so that he may honour the Immortals and build temples for us. And after a little time he shall die and go down to the realm of my brother Hades, and be subject to him.'

Prometheus did as he was told. He went to a place in Greece called Panopeus, not many miles to the north-east of Delphi, and from the red clay he fashioned Man. Then Zeus gave life to the clay men, and left Prometheus to teach them all things needful.

'You may give such gifts as are suitable,' Zeus said, 'but you must not give them fire – for that belongs to the Immortals. If you disobey me in this matter, your fate shall be more terrible than that of all the other Titans put together!'

After this Zeus went away into the rocky land of Arcadia in the south of Greece and dwelt there for a while with the Star Maiden Maia. They lived in a cave on the beautiful Mount Cyllene, and there a marvellous child was born, whose name was Hermes.

None of the Immortals knew where Zeus had gone,

nor what he was up to: but Apollo learnt, and in a strange way.

Apollo owned a herd of the most magnificent cattle, and they were guarded for him by Helios, the Titan who drove the chariot of the Sun, and who could see all that happened on the earth during the day.

One morning he sent a message to Apollo: the cows had vanished! Last night they were grazing peacefully in a green valley of Arcadia, and today there was not a trace of them to be seen.

Full of rage, Apollo set out across Greece in search of them, uttering terrible threats against the thief, and promising wonderful rewards to anyone who could find the cattle.

In Arcadia he met a band of Satyrs, who were wild wood-dwellers, left over, perhaps, from the Golden Age. Now they were inclined to be stupid and cowardly, full of mischief, and out to have a good time at all costs. They had pointed ears and little horns on their heads, and their leader Silenus was fat and foolish.

'We'll find your cows!' puffed Silenus. 'You trust us, Lord Apollo, we're always ready to help, and our eyes are sharp – and we're afraid of nothing!'

'Good!' said Apollo in his lordly fashion. 'Find my cows, and I will reward you well!'

Apollo went on his way, and the Satyrs began their search up and down the valleys of Arcadia.

After much search, they found the cows' hoof-marks: but to their great surprise the tracks all pointed directly *towards* the grazing-ground from which they had been stolen!

'They're mad! They're bewitched!' cried Silenus at length. 'And some terrible creature must have driven them: look at his footmarks!'

The Satyrs crowded round and stared at the traces of the cattle-thief which were large and round and blurred, with neither toes nor heels, but strange scratches and lines criss-crossing one another.

As they stood talking, a sound came to them out of the hillside, a new and wonderful sound which at first filled them with terror. It was the sound of music, the rich, sweet strains of the lyre which is like a zither or small harp.

After much discussion and many attempts on the part of Silenus to run away and leave the other Satyrs to face the monster, they all began to make as much noise as they could just outside the cave from which the music came – and *from* which the tracks of the cows led.

'He'll come out! He'll come out!' yelled the Satyrs. 'And he'll be so frightened of us that if he's the cattle-thief, he'll fall down with terror as soon as he sees us!'

Hardly had they spoken, when the door of the cave opened slowly. Silenus got ready to run away, and the Satyrs followed his example. But instead of any fearsome monster, there came out of the cave a beautiful mountain-nymph.

'Wild creatures,' she said in her sweet, gentle voice, 'why are you making this noise, and frightening all of us who dwell in this pleasant land? I heard your crazy shouting, and the stamp of your feet in front of my cave, and on the hillside above it, and I came out to know why you disturb a poor nymph like this.'

'Do not be angry, beautiful nymph,' begged Silenus. 'We do not come here as enemies, meaning to hurt you. But that sound, that wonderful sound of strange music which excites us so – what is it, and who is making it?'

'Come, that's better,' smiled the nymph. 'You will learn by gentleness what you would never discover by force. Then know that I am Cyllene, the nymph of this mountain, and that I am the nurse to a son of Zeus, and the Star Nymph, Maia. His name is Hermes, and he is truly a wonderful child! He is only six days old, and yet he grows at an amazing speed. As for the sound you heard, it was the child playing a strange thing which he has made out of a dead creature which made no sound at all when it was alive!'

'A dead creature!' cried Silenus. 'Not a cow, by any chance?'

'What nonsense you talk!' said Cyllene scornfully. 'The dead creature was a tortoise: Hermes has used its shell, that's all. He's made a wonderful new musical instrument by stretching a piece of ox-hide across it, and then stringing it with cow-gut . . .'

Cyllene paused, realizing that she had said too much, and Silenus exclaimed triumphantly:

'There you are, he *is* the thief who has stolen Apollo's cattle!'

'Do you dare to call the son of Zeus a thief!' protested Cyllene. 'I tell you it's nonsense! A baby less than a week old doesn't go stealing cows! And I'll swear, by any oath you like, that there isn't a single cow in the cave.'

'Well, let's see this child, anyhow,' demanded Silenus, and Cyllene had no choice but to go and bring Hermes.

Meanwhile Apollo, searching far and wide, came to the further side of Mount Cyllene, and found there strange tracks just as the Satyrs had found. And while he was puzzling over them, he came upon an old man called Battus, and pointing to the tracks he questioned him:

'There have been cows passing this way, though the tracks lead mysteriously to the grazing-ground from which they have been stolen. Tell me, old man, have you seen them, and do you know where they are?'

Battus, not recognizing Apollo, replied: 'My son, I am old and I cannot see very well. But what I saw lately has surprised me exceedingly. Last night I was digging in my vineyard when the sun went down: and I was still there after blessed Selene had driven the Moon-chariot up into the sky. And in the silvery, shimmering light I saw, or thought I saw, a child driving a great herd of cattle. Sometimes he drove them backwards, and sometimes he pulled them after him by their tails; and he was for ever darting about them like a gleam of quick-silver. Yet on his feet he wore strange shoes made of plaited osier twigs: you can see the round marks of them over yonder.'

Apollo thanked old Battus, and hastened on the trail of the cattle, following the hoof-marks backwards now that he knew how they had been driven. Very soon he found them penned into a great cave; and though he was glad to have discovered them, his brows darkened with anger when he saw that two of them were missing.

Penning the cattle in the cave behind him, Apollo followed the tracks across Mount Cyllene, and on the further side came upon the Satyrs who were still questioning Hermes outside Maia's cave.

'Lord Apollo!' cried Silenus excitedly. 'Here's the thief who stole your cows! This boy here! He's the son of Zeus, so he says: but he's a thief none the less. We've tracked two of the cows to this cave, and he has in his hand a piece of the skin of one of them!'

Apollo saw then that there would be trouble, so he hastily thanked Silenus and his Satyrs, gave them their reward, and sent them away.

Then he turned upon the little boy who sat, smiling innocently, in the sunshine, playing with his lyre, and said:

'Child, tell me quickly where my cattle are, or I shall

deal severely with you, and fling you down into Tartarus – even if you are indeed the son of Zeus.'

'Brother Apollo,' answered Hermes, looking up at the shining Immortal with big, wondering eyes, 'why do you speak to me so harshly? And why do you come here seeking for cattle? I have not seen them: how should I even know what cows look like? I am only a baby still: I do not care for anything but sleep, and warm milk; to lie wrapped in a warm cradle, or to play with toys such as this in my hand. But if it pleases you, I will swear an oath by Styx, the Black River of Death, for I am an Immortal even as you are, and I know that Immortals cannot break that oath. Listen: by Styx I swear that none of your cows are in this cave, and that I have not set eyes on the thief who stole them!'

Then Apollo smiled at the cunning of the child Hermes, and said: 'Surely after this your name shall be Prince of Robbers! But your clever story does not deceive me, so come quickly to Olympus, and if Zeus our father has returned, we will lay the case before him.'

He made as if to seize the child by the scruff of his neck, but before he could do so, Hermes laid his fingers gently upon the strings of his lyre and as the heavenly music swelled up, Apollo's hand fell to his side, and he stood still in amazement and delight.

Very soon, as he listened, he forgot his anger, and thought no more about his cows. His only desire was to make such music himself, and he stretched out his hands to Hermes:

'Give me the lyre!' he cried, 'and I will forgive you for the theft of my cattle, and for the two cows which you have killed. Give me the lyre, and swear that you will not steal from me again, and I will give you also my wand and make you the Herald of the Immortals, and the Guide of souls down the steep ways of death.'

As Apollo was speaking, Zeus drew near and heard all that he had said.

'It shall be so!' he cried in his voice of thunder. 'Swear the oath, son Hermes, and give the lyre to Apollo. Then shall he be the Lord of Music and of all sweet songs, and the Nine Muses shall follow him and do him honour. And you, Hermes, shall be our Messenger, right welcome in the golden halls of Olympus, and kindly disposed to the mortals upon earth.'

The oath was sworn, and Apollo took the lyre and went gladly on his way to Mount Helicon, where the Muses awaited him. When he grew tired of singing, he crossed to Parnassus, the next mountain, and that became his especial dwelling-place; and he slew the great serpent called Python who lived in a cave at lovely Delphi on its lowest slope. There, later on, stood the most famous of all the temples of Apollo in Greece, and there was his Oracle at which the priestess spoke the truest prophecies of the future in all the known world.

Hermes remained for a time in Arcadia; but he did not stay many days in the cave on Mount Cyllene, though Zeus lingered there with lovely Maia. Just as he had grown to boyhood in six days, so in a very brief space of time he was full-grown, and ready to seek a wife.

He had not far to search, for in a valley near by a nymph, Dryope, tended her sheep, and Hermes loved her at first sight. But Dryope was shy, frightened of the shining youth who came wooing her, and she declared that she would only marry a shepherd.

Hermes went away, but returned in disguise, bringing with him a flock of sheep – which, doubtless, he had stolen as easily as he had the cattle of Apollo. For a long time he grazed his sheep in the rich valleys, and met Dryope there from time to time, so that they became friends, and at last she consented to marry the supposed shepherd.

All went well for them in happy Arcadia, where the Golden Age seemed still to linger. But when Dryope's baby was born, she took one look at the child, and fled away shrieking. For the little creature had the legs and horns of a goat, and was born with a beard on his chin. All the same he was a noisy, merry, laughing child, and Hermes took him in his arms with delight, wrapped him in the soft skins of the wild hares, and carried him to Olympus.

Zeus had just returned, and he welcomed Hermes, and smiled at the strange child. All the other Immortals were pleased too with the merry little creature and they named him Pan and bade Hermes take him back to Arcadia. That was to be his chief dwelling-place, and there he was to attend to the flocks and herds, and to all wild things. When he grew older, Pan cut himself reeds in the river, and made the syrinx, the Pan-pipes, on which he played with a strange and mystical sweetness.

Zeus had little time to see how the son of Hermes would fare, for he had not been back in Olympus for long, when, looking out over the world after sundown, he beheld little sparks of light in many places; and in the daytime he saw smoke rising from the houses of newly-created men.

Then he knew that Prometheus the good Titan had disobeyed his orders and given fire to Mankind.

CHAPTER THREE

THE STORY OF PROMETHEUS

Lo, a god in the anguish, a god in the chain!
  The god, Zeus hateth sore
  And his gods hate again,
As many as tread on his glorified floor,
Because I loved mortals too much evermore.

AESCHYLUS
Prometheus Bound (Translated by
Elizabeth Barrett Browning)

3

After he had formed men out of the clay of Panopeus, and they had received the breath of life from Zeus, Prometheus set to work to make them something more than mere living images of the gods.

For Man as first created was little better than the beasts, a poor creature, who did not know how to think or how to use the things which he saw and felt round about him. He lived in caves, ate herbs and raw meat: and when he was wounded or ill, he died because he knew nothing of medicine or surgery.

But Prometheus, the good and kind, taught men all the

arts and crafts of life. He taught them how to build houses and make tools; how to plough the earth and sow the corn, how to reap it when it had grown, to thresh out the bright grains and grind them between flat stones. He showed them how to catch and tame some of the wild creatures: the dog to guard their houses and go hunting with them; the horse to draw their chariots, and the ox to pull the plough; the sheep to yield wool, and the goats' milk which might be made into cheese.

It is said that Prometheus also gave men the power of speech, taught them the names of all things and even how to write and read.

But it was slow work, since Fire, the greatest aid, was missing. Without it meat must still be eaten raw, and tools could be made only of stone; bread could not be baked, and the house could not be warmed in winter.

Prometheus looked up at the sun, coursing across the sky in the golden chariot which Helios drove, and he sighed deeply. For he could read the future, and though much of it remained dark to him, what he could see he knew would surely happen.

Then he called to him his brother Epimetheus, who was as foolish, thoughtless, and improvident as he was wise, thoughtful, and fore-sighted.

'My brother,' he said. 'You have helped me so far, and now you live as a man among men to carry on my work. You know how well I love the men whom we have made and taught – and yet you, who see only the outward aspect of everything, do not realize how deep such a love as mine can be. Listen! I must give Fire to mankind, the last and greatest of gifts. But if I do so, I shall incur the terrible wrath of Zeus . . . Yet even that I will endure – for so it is ordained. But I beg you to guard mankind to the best of your power, and to be very careful when I am no longer with you. Above all things, beware of any gift from Zeus.'

Then Prometheus bade farewell to his brother, and set out for Olympus, carrying with him the stalk of a fennel plant, as long as a staff and hard as wood, but hollow and filled with a white pith which would burn slowly and steadily like the wick of a candle.

At the foot of Olympus he was met by Athena, the Immortal daughter of Zeus, the Lady of Wisdom, who had helped Prometheus in his labours for mankind. There was a strange story told of her birth, which shows that her father Zeus might have taken after the terrible Titans such as Cronos.

For while Zeus was still at war with the Titans, he married Metis, daughter of the friendly Titan, Ocean, and Prometheus came to him and said:

'Mighty Zeus, if Metis bears you a child, it will be stronger and wiser than you, its father!'

Then Zeus, who knew that whatever Prometheus prophesied was certain to be true, was much alarmed. Metis had all the terrible powers of the Titans, and at that time Zeus was not yet armed with his thunderbolts; but he thought of a clever plan, or maybe Prometheus thought of it for him.

'Lady Metis,' he said, 'I know that you have the wonderful power of turning yourself into any creature you please. I can well believe that you could become a great and magnificent animal such as a lioness or a she-bear; but surely it is beyond your power to turn yourself into so small and worthless a creature as a fly!'

'Beyond my power, is it?' cried Metis, forgetting her usual prudence. 'I'll show you!' And in a moment she had turned herself into a fly. Zeus smiled, caught the fly – and swallowed it.

That was the end of Metis, and by swallowing her Zeus added all her wisdom to his own, also her power of shape-shifting. But some months later a terrible pain shot through his head, and grew worse and worse, until he cried out in agony for Prometheus to help him.

Prometheus took his axe and split open the head of Zeus, knowing that an Immortal cannot die, and being himself the master of the art of healing.

Then a great wonder was seen, for from the head of Zeus sprang Athena the daughter of Metis, fully grown and clad in shining armour. She had the wisdom of Metis also, but had no wish to surpass her father Zeus. Her wisdom was of a gentler kind, so that she became the teacher of such arts as spinning and weaving, and also of good and wise government. But she had some of her mother's fierceness also, as she proved by joining in the battle at her father's side, and slaying the Titan Pallas, whose skin she flayed off to make her cloak and whose name she added to her own, so that all who were unjust might fear the terrible voice of Pallas Athena. She could be jealous too, as she proved when the mortal maiden Arachne boasted that her skill in weaving was greater than Athena's, for, not content with proving her superiority by a contest, Athena turned the foolish girl into a spider – to weave cobwebs and useless gossamer.

But Athena was always friendly to Prometheus, and interested in his work for mankind; and so when she knew that he had decided to give them Fire, she led him by the secret paths to the summit of Olympus.

As day drew to an end, Helios drove up in his shining chariot, and Prometheus, hiding by the gateway, needed but to stretch out his fennel-stalk and touch the golden wheel. Then, the precious spark concealed under his cloak, he hastened down the mountain side, and away into a deep valley of Arcadia where he heaped up a pile of wood and kindled it.

The first people upon earth to see the wonderful new gift of fire were the wild Satyrs who dwelt in the lonely valleys. Slowly and shyly they gathered round the edge of the glade in which Prometheus had lighted the first camp-fire; and gradually they drew nearer and nearer.

'Oh the lovely thing!' they cried as they felt the warmth.

'How beautifully it dances; how warm, and gentle, and comforting this new creature is!'

'Oh how I love it!' cried Silenus. 'It shall be mine, mine! See, I will kiss the lovely creature, to prove it!'

With that he knelt down and tried to kiss the tallest and brightest tongue of flame. The look on his face was so comical as the flame scorched him and burnt his beard, that Prometheus sat back and roared with laughter.

But he had more serious work in hand, and when day dawned he began to teach men the uses of Fire. He showed them how to cook meat and bake bread; how to make bronze and smelt iron; how to hammer the hot metals into swords and plough-shares, and all the other cunning crafts of the smith and the metal-worker.

Now that Fire had come upon the Earth, fire could be kindled there whenever it was needed. So Prometheus, with the help of Hermes, invented rubbing-sticks and taught men which woods to use and how to twirl the hard piece in the soft until fire was kindled by the friction.

So mankind came into his true inheritance: cities began to grow up, and men to practise all the arts and crafts for which Greece was soon to become famous.

But Zeus, as soon as he became aware that his command had been disobeyed and the gift which he withheld had been stolen and given to men, summoned Prometheus before him.

'Titan!' he cried fiercely. 'You have disobeyed me! What

is there to prevent me from casting you down into Tartarus with your brethren, and destroying these vile insects, these men, to whom you have given gifts reserved for the Immortals alone?'

'Lord Zeus,' answered Prometheus quietly, 'I know what is to come, and how cruelly you will punish me for all I have done. But there are two things you cannot do: no Immortal may take away the gift an Immortal has once given – so you will not deprive men of fire now that I have made it theirs. And I am certain that you will not destroy mankind, when I tell you that a man – your son, born of a mortal woman – will save you and all of you who dwell in Olympus on that future day when Earth will bring forth the Giants meaning to be revenged for the overthrow of the Titans. This I tell you, and you know that my words are true: no Immortal can slay a Giant, but a Man can slay them, if he be strong and brave enough. And I will tell you this also: at a certain time in the future you will fall as your father fell.'

Then the wrath of Zeus was terrible. In a voice of thunder he bade his son Hephaestus, the Immortal whose skill was in the working of metals, take Prometheus and bind him with fetters of brass to the great mountain of Caucasus on the eastern edge of the world.

'There you shall lie,' he cried in his cruel rage, 'for ever and ever as a punishment for your daring and disobedience. The snows of winter will freeze you, and the summer sun will burn you: and your fate shall be a warning to all who would disobey!'

Then sorrowfully Hephaestus took Prometheus, and at his command his two servants, the demons Might and Force, chained him to the rock with fetters that he could not break.

But as Hephaestus was about to leave him there, Prometheus said:

'Zeus, that cruel tyrant, will fall as Cronos fell, unless he can find out how to avert his doom. And how to do that, I alone know!'

Hephaestus reported these words, and Hermes was sent to offer Prometheus his freedom if he would tell the secret.

'If you do not at once disclose what you know,' said Hermes, 'Zeus will torture you until you do so. He will send a fierce eagle who will visit you every day and devour your liver: and every night your liver will grow again so that next day your agonies may be repeated.'

Still Prometheus would not say how Zeus could avoid the fate which hung over him, and, though the eagle did as Zeus had threatened, still he would not tell. But at times his screams echoed over the haunted cliffs and chasms of Caucasus, so that none dared to approach.

Meanwhile Zeus, a prey to fears for the future, and still made cruel by terror, sought how he might plague mankind so that the gift of fire might not make them too happy.

Now at first men had full knowledge of their own future, and Zeus, not knowing that Prometheus, with his great foresight, had taken this power from them, decided to make them immortal also, so that when he had worked his will on them and set free sin and care in the world, they might go mad with terror knowing the sorrows and sufferings which lay in store for them.

He went cunningly to work, visiting men in disguise and asking who had given them the gift of Fire.

And men betrayed their benefactor, Prometheus, with cruel thoughtlessness. This gave Zeus his excuse: 'I will reward you,' he said, 'for telling me what I wanted to know, by giving you a jar of nectar, the drink of the Immortals, which keeps them for ever young.'

The men who received this precious gift were overjoyed; but with the usual folly and laziness of mankind, they put it on the back of a donkey and drove it before them towards a place where they meant to keep it in safety. Presently they came to a spring of clear water bubbling from the rock, and when they had refreshed themselves, they sat down to eat at a little distance, leaving the donkey to graze near by.

Soon the donkey felt thirsty too, and went over to the spring for a drink. But now there was a cunning snake guarding it, who spoke to the donkey with crafty words.

'If you touch my spring, I will bite you, and you will die in agony from the poison.'

'I am dying already – of thirst' – protested the donkey. 'So please let me drink a little of the cool spring water.'

'Well,' said the guileful Serpent, 'I'll make a bargain with you. Give me the wine in the jar on your back. It's warm, and nasty, and donkeys don't like wine, anyway. If you give it to me, I'll let you drink as much water from my cool, refreshing spring as you please.'

'Agreed,' cried the donkey eagerly, and the exchange was made – and that is why snakes renew their youth every year, casting off the old skin and appearing as young and shining as ever.

When Zeus discovered that men could no longer foresee the future, he was rather pleased that the snake had cheated the donkey: for he knew that in the days to come many serpents would bite both men and asses, and that snake-bite produces a worse fever of thirst than anything.

Meanwhile he was busy on a surer punishment for Man: he was making the first Woman. Her name was Pandora, which means 'all-gifted', for all of the Immortals helped to endow her. Clever Hephaestus shaped her out of clay, and lovely Aphrodite gave her beauty, while Hermes taught her cunning and boldness, and Athena dressed her in lovely clothes. Zeus breathed life into her, and then Hermes led her down to earth and brought her to Epimetheus, the thoughtless brother of Prometheus, who lived now more or less as a man among men.

When Epimetheus saw the beauty of Pandora he forgot

his brother's warning against accepting any gift from Zeus, and fell in love with her at once. Very soon they were married, and they had a daughter called Pyrrha, who married Deucalion, the wisest and most virtuous of all the First Men whom Prometheus had fashioned out of clay.

But meanwhile Pandora brought all the evil upon mankind which Zeus had planned.

In the house of Epimetheus stood a golden box which Prometheus had left there with strict orders that no one was to open it. Epimetheus told his wife this, but she was so curious and inquisitive that life did not seem worth living until she knew what treasure it was that her husband was hiding from her.

So one day when he was out, Pandora crept quietly to the golden casket and lifted the lid. Then with a rush and a cry out came all the ills which beset mankind – diseases, and sorrows, hate, jealousy, lies, theft, cheating, and a hundred others.

Terrified at what she had done, Pandora slammed down the lid. But a little voice cried: 'Let me out too! I am Hope!'

For Prometheus had placed Hope there when he shut up the evil things, so that mankind might not suffer quite so much if Zeus had his way.

CHAPTER FOUR

How Zeus and Hermes Went Visiting

The gods are angry: we shall never be
Now as of old, when far from all men we
  Dwelt in a lonely land and languorous,
Circled and sundered by the sleeping sea.

Yea, the Olympians then were wont to go
Among us, visible godheads, to and fro.

J.W. MACKAIL
In Scheria

4

Time went by and men settled down all over the earth as if it had always been theirs. And Zeus was pleased with what he saw as he looked down from Olympus, and busied himself setting the rest of the world to rights after the desolation made by the Titans.

Of course it was to Greece that he gave most of his attention, though he did not neglect the islands of the Aegean Sea which separates Greece from Asia Minor, nor that part of the mainland beyond which is called Troy.

When he was tired with his labours, Zeus would go southwards to the land of the Blessed Ethiopians, men of the Silver Age who had not learnt the wickedness of the Titans, and who often entertained the Immortals at their banquets.

But the evils which Pandora had let loose from the golden casket found their way surely enough into the hearts of men, and some even in Greece became almost as wicked as those of the Silver Age whom Zeus had destroyed before Prometheus made Man as we know him out of clay.

Rumours of wickedness beyond belief came to Zeus, and he began to wonder whether he could destroy the people of the Bronze Age and make yet another race of men: but without Prometheus to help him, he hesitated. At last he decided to see for himself, and so he called to him his son Hermes and said:

'Let us take upon ourselves the form and likeness of men and go down into the land of Greece and seek entertainment as if we were poor travellers. And if we find that men are not fit to live upon the beautiful earth, I will destroy them utterly.'

Hermes, who loved mankind and had helped Prometheus, replied:

'Father Zeus, let us not be over hasty. If we visit three households, and find that two out of the three merit destruction, then let mankind perish. But if we find virtue and kindness in even two, however wicked the third may be, then spare the good. But bring whatever doom you like upon the wicked.'

This pleased Zeus, who had grown less cruel than in the days when he sent Prometheus to his terrible doom and made Pandora to be a plague to all mankind.

He agreed to what Hermes suggested, and the two Immortals began their wanderings in the land of Arcadia, Zeus disguised as an old man and Hermes as his grandson.

Now at that time the King of Arcadia was Lycaon, a fierce, savage man given to all manner of evil. He had fifty sons, and most of them were as bad as he was, and like him they were cannibals.

Zeus and Hermes entered King Lycaon's palace, and at first he refused to give them food, and even threatened to kill them. Hermes so young and handsome would make him an excellent feast; perhaps it was this which made him change his mind.

Certainly he bade Zeus sit down at his table: perhaps he considered Hermes already a prisoner being fattened up for a future banquet. Suddenly Lycaon realized that there was no fresh meat ready for that day; but this did not trouble him over much, since he had one son, Nyctimus, who was not as wicked as the rest, and always refused to eat human flesh. On this day he had dared to tell his father that to eat one of his guests was the wickedest thing a man could do.

'You're only fit for stewing!' snarled Lycaon; and so Nyctimus was killed, jointed, and put in the pot.

When this hideous meal was placed on the table, Zeus the all-seeing knew at once what the dish was which was set before him. Filled with rage he sprang to his feet, and a great light shone round him as Lycaon cowered away, realizing in a moment of terror that his guest was none other than the King of the Immortals.

'Wretch!' cried Zeus. 'All that I have heard of you is true! You are not fit to be a man! Go forth into the wilderness and haunt the lonely mountains and dangerous valleys: be a wolf, and your impious sons with you!'

Then Lycaon tried to answer, but all he could utter was the howl of a wolf. He tried to fall upon his knees, only to find that he was already on all fours. So he fled away into the forests of Arcadia with his sons behind him, a wolf at the head of his pack.

Zeus restored Nyctimus to life and bade him rule justly and well. Then he and Hermes, once more in disguise, continued on their way.

'You see,' said Zeus presently. 'Men are as wicked as I thought. Is there need of further search?'

'Remember your promise,' answered Hermes. 'And this time, let us seek hospitality of a poor man: perhaps we may find a virtue among the humble which is lacking to a king such as Lycaon.'

So they went on across the world, passing at will over sea and land, and came in the evening to a mountain top near Tyana in Phrygia. Here stood a little cottage thatched with straw, and the walls made of reeds and clay. There were no servants in this house, indeed its only inhabitants were an old man and his wife whose names were Philemon and Baucis.

Poor though they were, these two welcomed the travellers kindly, made up the fire with their last dry faggot, put on the pot to boil, and cut up their only joint of smoked bacon which hung from the beam.

They prepared a bed for their guests, the only bed in the house, and heaped all the rugs they possessed upon it. Then they laid the table and set the supper before the two strangers.

Besides the meat there were olives and cheese; eggs roasted in the warm embers, and what little store they had of dried figs, dates, and nuts. Old Baucis, her hands trembling with age, served the meal, while Philemon placed two wooden cups upon the table and poured into them wine from the only jar that remained to him.

All this they did with simple kindness, talking to their guests and making them welcome, without the slightest idea that they were anything but human travellers as poor as themselves.

But when Philemon came to re-fill the cups which he had seen his guests drain to the dregs, he found them both still full of wine – and of wine so sweet and fragrant that the delicious scent of it filled the whole cottage. Then he fell on his knees before the guests:

'Noble sirs,' he cried, holding up his hands in prayer, 'surely you are blessed gods come down from Olympus! Pardon us, I beg you, that our entertainment has been so poor, and the food so meagre. Indeed, we would have done better, if we possessed better: but we have given you all we had.'

Then Zeus smiled kindly on the two old people, and said:

'You have guessed truly: we are Zeus and Hermes, come down to test mankind – and in you we find nothing to blame. Come now, and see what we propose for you!'

He led the way out of the cottage, and scarcely had they left it when it began to grow and change as they watched it. The rough sticks which held up the roof turned into columns of white marble; the thatch grew yellower and yellower until it shone with pure gold, and the dark earthen floor grew hard and smooth with many-coloured mosaic.

'And now,' said Zeus, 'what gift do you desire for yourselves?'

Then Philemon and Baucis spoke together for a few moments, after which Philemon turned and said:

'Of all things we desire most to be your priest and priestess in the beautiful temple which you have made. And this also we beg, that since we have lived our lives together in such perfect harmony and happiness, we may both die at the same moment.'

'All this I grant,' cried Zeus, and the thunder rolled

across the sky in token of his gift. 'And, whatever may chance to the wicked among men, here on this sacred mountain top you will be safe. Moreover I make you young again: live your lives as virtuously as you have done, and when death comes to you, both on the instant shall be turned into trees that you may still stand here and bow your heads before my temple.'

So saying, Zeus turned away from Baucis and Philemon, and set out once more with Hermes, in the direction of Greece.

Soon they came to wooded Thessaly in the north of Greece, and here Zeus turned to Hermes and said:

'Son of Maia, we have found a virtuous and holy couple living in Asia, but here in our own land of Greece Lycaon the impious man-eater, the wolf-king. This our last visit will save or destroy mankind!'

Now it may be that Hermes knew, and led the way, or it may be that Zeus was anxious for an excuse to spare some at least of the race of men: but certain it is that the house in which they next sought shelter was that of Deucalion whom Prometheus had made from the clay of Panopeus, and his wife Pyrrha, the daughter of Epimetheus and Pandora.

They found these two everything that they could wish: kindly and pious, honouring the gods, living blameless lives, and practising diligently all the arts which Prometheus had taught.

'Now,' said Zeus, when he and Hermes had tested Deucalion's hospitality and found that a King of Thessaly could be as simple and kindly as an ancient peasant of Phrygia – 'Now I will return to Olympus, and let loose a great flood over the earth. All those who are not fit to live shall drown in that flood, and I will see to it that any who save themselves by climbing to the tops of mountains are worthy of life – and I fear there will be few indeed of them. As for you, noble Deucalion, make haste and build a ship; place a roof over the top of it, store food and clothes in it, and then enter it with your wife and children. In this ship you will be safe, and I will guide it to the land over which I purpose that you and your children shall rule.'

Then Deucalion did as he was bidden, and brought to the task all the skill which Prometheus had taught him. Soon the ship was finished, and as soon as he and Pyrrha were safely inside it, Zeus let loose the rain.

For nine days and nine nights the rain poured down upon the earth; and Poseidon stirred up the waves with his trident so that the sea flowed in over the land as well.

All was desolation: houses lay in ruins beneath the waters, the corn rotted and turned black, and the fishes swam in and out among the branches of the trees. Only the Sea-peoples, the Nymphs and the Dolphins, were happy, swimming about among the mountain tops, and diving down to explore drowned cities beneath the waves.

At last the waters began to fall, and the ship came to rest on a slope of Mount Parnassus, near Apollo's shrine at Delphi. Praising the gods for their deliverance, Deucalion and Pyrrha stepped on shore and lay down to sleep.

In the morning a voice spoke to them out of the deep earth beneath Apollo's temple which was now hung with sea-weed and encrusted with shells:

'Deucalion and Pyrrha! Father Zeus does not mean to stamp out utterly the race of men. Therefore go down into the valley before you, cover your heads with your cloaks, and cast behind you the bones of your mother!'

For a long time they were puzzled by this command, for each of them had a different mother, and both were dead. But at last Deucalion hit upon the right answer:

'Surely,' he said, 'our mother is the Earth, for out of earth were men formed by our maker Prometheus. And the bones of earth must be the stones.'

So they went down into the river valley, covered their heads, and began to throw stones backwards over their shoulders. And presently as they threw they heard a murmur behind them, a murmur that swelled and swelled until at last they could restrain themselves no longer.

They turned round, and there was a multitude of men and women. And as they gazed they saw the last few stones which they had thrown swelling, changing, growing soft and rising up into human shapes: the men from the stones which Deucalion had thrown and the women from those which fell behind Pyrrha.

In this way the land of Greece was re-peopled, and very soon new cities sprang up from the ruins of the old; the fields yielded rich corn once more, and the olive groves shimmered silver in the sunlight.

So earth was peopled anew, and the children of Deucalion and Pyrrha, with those who had survived the flood by climbing to the mountain tops, became the kings and queens of the various states of Greece; and the most famous of them, whose name was Hellen, gave his name to the whole country, which is often called Hellas to this very day, and its people the Hellenes.

Zeus was pleased with mankind now that the more evil of them had been destroyed, and he and the other Immortals wandered often through the lovely land of Hellas, and some married mortal brides whose children became kings and princes.

'This is the Age of the Heroes,' decreed Zeus, 'and the men in it shall be stronger and the women more beautiful than their descendants in times to come.' For Zeus remembered the prophecy of the Titan Prometheus, that when the Giants came to attack him and the other Immortals, they could only win the war if there was a mortal man strong and brave enough to fight at their side and kill the Giants when they had overthrown them.

So Zeus planned, hoping that the greatest Hero of all would be born in time to help him. The Heroic Age lasted until the contemporaries of the youngest son of that Hero had grown old and died, and among them was Odysseus, the last of the Heroes who fought at Troy.

But, without the wisdom of Prometheus to guide him, Zeus made a mistake which very nearly caused his doom and wrecked the world. For when Deucalion and Pyrrha had made men and women by casting stones over their shoulders, Zeus, eager to make Greece a pleasant dwelling-place for the Heroes, laid command upon Earth.

'Bring forth Animals!' he commanded, for all animal life had perished in the great flood, though the birds and the reptiles had been able to survive it.

Earth did as she was bidden, and animals of every kind came leaping and tumbling out of the ground, squeezing up between the rocks, and pushing their way through the ground just as a mole does. But she laughed to herself, deep down in the caverns where the Titans were imprisoned. And besides the animals, she made the Giants – though they did not come out of their caves for a long time yet to do battle with the Immortals. But in addition to the Giants, Earth produced the most fearful monster ever seen, who was called Typhon.

CHAPTER FIVE

TYPHON THE TERRIBLE

The lyre's voice is lovely everywhere;
In the courts of gods, in the city of men,
And in the lonely rock-strewn mountain-glen,
In the still mountain air.

Only to Typhon it sounds hatefully;
To Typhon only, the rebel o'erthrown,
Through whose heart Etna drives her roots of
  stone,
To imbed them in the sea.

MATTHEW ARNOLD
Empedocles on Etna

5

Typhon, the last of the Titans, was born out of the Earth in Asia Minor, far away from the sight of Zeus. Earth hid him as long as possible in a great dark cave in a place called Cilicia, that he might be full-grown before Zeus discovered about him.

But when Typhon came to full size, there was no hiding for him anywhere in the world. Of all creatures ever known upon the earth, he was the biggest and most frightful.

He was so tall that as he walked far out in the sea the waves came only a little way above his knees; and when he stood upon the dry land, the stars became entangled in his hair. He was terrible to look at, for from his shoulders grew a hundred heads, with dark, flickering serpent tongues and flaming eyes. Each head uttered from its fearsome mouth a voice of its own: some spoke in words that men could understand, but others bellowed like bulls, or roared like lions or howled like hunting wolves. From this monster's shoulders grew dragons' wings; and his hands were so strong that he could lift mountains with them.

As soon as he was grown to his full height, Typhon came striding suddenly across the Aegean Sea towards Greece, roaring with rage like a thousand hurricanes. Straight for Olympus he came, for the one thought in each of his hundred heads was to destroy the Immortals and rule in their place.

Then there was terror and panic in heaven, and to save themselves the Immortals fled away into the land of Egypt where they disguised themselves by assuming the heads of animals or birds so that Typhon might not know them. The Egyptians made statues of them and gave them new names: Artemis with a cat's head they called Bast; Dionysus with the ram's head became Osiris, cow-headed Demeter became Isis, and so on with the other Immortals.

But Zeus did not flee: he stood up on Olympus to do battle with his fearful enemy, and hurled a thunderbolt at him.

Typhon laughed at thunderbolts, and catching the next

one Zeus threw he hurled it back, and after that a whole cascade of rocks and mountain tops.

Zeus dodged them, and snatched up the great sickle made of adamant with which in the beginning of time Cronos had maimed his father the Sky. With this weapon, harder and sharper than the sharpest iron, he attacked the monster, and the whole earth shook and quaked as they fought. Long and fiercely the battle raged; but Zeus was the stronger, and soon Typhon was bleeding from many wounds.

But as they rolled on the ground, wrestling and struggling together, Typhon made one last tremendous effort and wrenched the sickle from Zeus, while he twined the snakey coils of his body round him and held him prisoner for a moment. Then with a few swift blows Typhon cut off the immortal sinews from Zeus's arms and legs, leaving him lying on the slope of Olympus, powerless to move.

Typhon also was sorely wounded and bleeding from many cuts, but he managed to crawl down into a deep valley in the wild land of Thrace in northern Greece, and hid the sinews deep in a cave. Then he rested outside in the sun, guarding the sinews, and waiting until his wounds healed and his strength came back to him.

Meanwhile Hermes and Pan came quietly across the world in search of Zeus, and found him lying on the mountain side, unable to stir, powerless to defend himself if Typhon returned to the attack.

They thought of many schemes to save him, and at last Hermes devised a plan:

'We need some simple human to help us,' he said. 'Typhon is an Immortal himself, so that he would recognize either of us, however well we disguised ourselves.'

Then Zeus remembered that Prince Cadmus was at this moment wandering among the hills of Thrace in search of his sister Europa.

For it happened that a little while before the coming of Typhon, Zeus had visited the land of Phoenicia, to the north of Palestine, in the shape of a wonderful white bull with horns of gold.

The Princess Europa had been playing on the sea-shore with her companions, and she was delighted with the beauty of the white bull. At first she was afraid, but it came to her in such a friendly way, and let her stroke it, that soon she was treating it almost as a pet. She twined garlands of flowers for its horns, and then, much daring, climbed on to its back for a ride. The white bull was gentleness itself: he walked carefully up and down the beach, and then began to splash through the little waves as they broke on the sandy shore. At first Europa was wild with delight, but her excitement changed suddenly to fear when the bull moved into deep water, and began to swim out to sea.

She screamed vainly for help, and clung desperately to the golden horns; but the bull brought her safely across the sea to the island of Crete. There Zeus resumed his ordinary shape, and told her that her children should rule in this beautiful island, and so well and so wisely that after their death two of her sons would be made judges of the souls of the dead in the realm of Hades.

But meanwhile, in Phoenicia, the King, Europa's father, called his three sons to him and said:

'Go north and south and west in search of your sister, and do not return without her, or you shall die!'

That was why the eldest of them, Prince Cadmus, was wandering through the valleys of Thrace in northern Greece when suddenly the two Immortals met him.

'Do not be afraid, Prince Cadmus,' said Hermes, 'we bring you a message from Zeus. You shall be king of a great city in Greece, and your children shall be famous. Zeus will be your friend, and heap good things upon you and yours . . . But now he himself is in terrible need, and you can help him.'

They disguised Cadmus as a shepherd, and Hermes built a little house for him not far from where Typhon was. Pan, the kindly goat-footed Immortal who has charge of all shepherds and their flocks, lent Cadmus some sheep, and gave him also his wonderful pipes which play sweeter, more magical tunes than any made by mortal hands.

And when Hermes had instructed him in all that he must say and do, Prince Cadmus, in his disguise, went wandering down the valley playing upon the pipes of Pan, with the sheep and lambs gambolling and frisking about him. Presently he came to where Typhon was lying on the soft grass in front of his cave. Typhon heard the music, and made no attempt to harm the simple shepherd who could breathe through the pipes such sweet and wonderful sounds.

'Do not be afraid of me, shepherd,' rumbled the monster, 'but play and let me hear sweeter music still, so that I may forget my pains and grow whole more speedily. And when I am lord of heaven and earth I will reward you royally.'

So Cadmus set the pipes of Pan to his lips once more and played the wild, sweet notes such as come from no other pipes in the world. And Typhon felt that never in his life had he heard anything so wonderful.

'Play! Play again!' he cried eagerly as Cadmus paused for breath.

'So you like the tune of my pipes,' said Cadmus. 'If only you could hear the music of my lyre, you would not even remember the pipes! Why, Apollo himself does not play upon the lyre so sweetly as I do.'

'Then play on the lyre, whatever that is,' grunted Typhon.

'Alas,' said Cadmus cunningly, 'I cannot do so any more. For when I played more sweetly than Apollo himself, that jealous master of music snatched the lyre from my hands and broke all the strings. See, here it is; and unless I can find fresh sinews with which to string it, I can never again draw from it the most beautiful music in the world.'

Suspecting no evil of this simple young shepherd who played so enchantingly, Typhon crawled painfully into his cave and presently returned carrying the sinews of Zeus.

'Here,' he rumbled. 'Take these! String them to your lyre, and play me to sleep!'

Cadmus took the sinews and placed them carefully in the hollow of the lyre under the stretched cow-hide which made the sounding-board.

'I will take these back to my cottage,' he said, 'and fit them in place tonight, so that tomorrow I may delight you with the lyre's melody. It is a slow and delicate task and will take time. But now let me play you a lullaby on the pipes.'

Then, without giving Typhon time to think, Cadmus played on the pipes of Pan a lullaby so soothing and so filled with the drowsy whispers of slumber that all his heads began to nod and his two hundred eyes to close. Soon he lay there asleep, his snores murmuring up the valley like distant thunder on a summer's night, and Cadmus crept swiftly away.

Beyond the hills Hermes and Pan were waiting for him, and while Hermes took the sinews and made haste to carry them to Zeus, Pan led Cadmus swiftly south, away and away until he came to the sea shore where his ship was waiting for him.

Zeus fitted the sinews back into his arms and legs once more, and in a moment his strength returned to him. He leapt into his chariot, caught up a handful of thunderbolts, and rode out to do battle again with his terrible enemy.

Typhon, still bleeding from his earlier encounter with Zeus, fled away this time in terror and, pelted with thunderbolts, he fell down at last and lay grovelling in the sea not far from Italy.

Then Zeus caught up the island of Sicily and flung it upon him. And there he lies imprisoned for ever under the roots of Mount Etna. Sometimes he still writhes, and cries out in fury, sending his fiery breath up through the volcano and with it streams of burning lava which lay waste the fair fields and vineyards of Sicily.

But meanwhile Prince Cadmus was sailing over the blue sea towards Delphi, for so Pan had told him to do, since by the command of Zeus he must seek for Europa no longer, but make ready to found a kingdom of his own.

Presently, when he had finished with Typhon, Zeus sent a storm which blew Cadmus's ship out of its course, away to the eastward, until on the tenth day it came to the enchanted island of Samothrace.

On this island stood a palace made of gold, with marble pillars and floors of precious stones. It was surrounded by the loveliest garden in the world, filled all the year round with every sort of flower and fruit, always in season.

Hephaestus, the Immortal Smith, had built this palace by the command of Zeus as a home for Harmonia, the daughter of Ares and Aphrodite; and there this fairy princess lived, with the nymph Electra to look after her, and Electra's children to guard her from all enemies. And the eldest of these children was Dardanus who later became the first king of Troy.

Electra welcomed Cadmus to her beautiful home and entertained him and his companions for many days. The lovely Harmonia walked in the fragrant gardens with the handsome young prince, and very soon they fell in love with one another, just as Zeus had intended.

Then one day Hermes came to Samothrace and said to Electra:

'Cadmus and Harmonia love one another, and Father Zeus, remembering his promise to the brave prince who did him such notable service in his battle with Typhon, has decreed that they be man and wife. So bid them set sail in the swift ship, with all their followers and attendants, and pass over the sea to Delphi as Zeus bids: for there the oracle of Apollo will tell Cadmus where to found his city.'

Electra did as she was told, and very soon the ship with white sails set was dancing over the blue waves, leaving behind an island which was no longer enchanted, now that Harmonia had left it.

They sailed over the summer seas among the jewel-like

islands of the Aegean. They passed round stormy Cape Malea at the south of Greece – but the kind sea-nymphs guided them past all the treacherous rocks, and a gentle wind wafted them speedily on their way.

At last they came up the lovely Gulf of Corinth, anchored the ship in a land-locked bay, and went up to Delphi the beautiful on its green and grey hillside beneath the yellow cliffs of Parnassus.

There Apollo spoke the will of Zeus through his oracle:

'Cadmus!' said the voice out of the streaming shadows of the dark cleft beneath the temple. 'Cadmus! You left your distant home to search for the White Bull of Zeus. Seek it no longer, but follow where a Cow shall lead; and where that Cow sinks to rest, build a city with seven gates and call it Thebes!'

Cadmus did as he was told; and down in the valley below Delphi he found the Cow grazing. As soon as it saw him coming it raised its head, lowed gently, and set off up the valley. Up the steep pass at the top it went, past the dark junction of three roads, and down the hillside beyond into the most fertile plain in all Greece.

When it came to the place appointed, it sank down to rest, and Cadmus knew that his quest was accomplished. It had stopped on a low ridge of land with a little valley on either side; and there Cadmus built his citadel, with walls and a palace and temples.

When the palace and the walls round the citadel were complete; and Cadmus had killed the dragon which lived below the hill, and had marked out fields and rich corn lands for his followers, he held his wedding to Harmonia.

To that Wedding Feast came all the Immortals from Olympus. Zeus himself sat at the head of the table, with Hera beside him; Ares and Aphrodite were there, of course, to give away their daughter as bride to the brave prince who had won her. Hermes and Pan were there, and Apollo to make music with his heavenly lyre while the Nine Muses sang the marriage hymn, and Immortals made merry with mortal men and women.

When the feast was ended the Immortals returned to Olympus, and only once again, as shall be told, did they come to the wedding of a mortal man.

Cadmus and Harmonia lived happily all their lives; and when the time came for them to die, Zeus carried them away to the Elysian Fields where it is always spring. There they dwell for ever unchanging, with the shades of those men and women whom Zeus has chosen for this immortality.

CHAPTER SIX

THE ADVENTURES OF DIONYSUS

Semele dared a wish, – to see;
That her eyes might equal be
With her heart and lips and ears:
Night on perfect night she pled.
Sudden lightning drank her tears,
Life and sweetness: she lay dead.

T. STURGE MOORE
Semele

6

After the struggle with Typhon, Zeus began to look out more and more anxiously for the Hero who was to help him defeat the Giants. If Earth could still produce a monster like Typhon, the war with the Giants might be much nearer than he thought!

It may have been due to something which Prometheus had said, or to some half-knowledge of his own, but Zeus became certain that the Hero would be born at Thebes.

So when Cadmus and Harmonia had built their city of the seven gates, with the aid of the musicians Amphion and Zethus (at the sound of whose lyre the stones moved of themselves to make the walls) Zeus took good note of their children.

The eldest of these was Autonoe; but when she married, her only son, Actaeon, came to a tragic end. He insulted Artemis, the Immortal Huntress, boasting one day when he found her bathing in a lonely pool on Mount Cithaeron that he was a better huntsman than she would ever be. In her anger she turned him into a stag, and he was hunted by his own hounds, who caught him and tore him to pieces without knowing what they did.

Next came Ino, who married Athamas, king of a city not far from Thebes, who already had two children, Phrixus and Helle. Their mother was Nephele the Cloud Maiden; and after they were born, she flew back to heaven, and Athamas never saw her again. When Ino had children of her own she hated these two who were not quite as other mortals, and soon showed herself to be a cruel and wicked stepmother. She dared not kill them herself, but by parching the seed-corn secretly she caused a famine, and then bribed the messenger who was sent to Delphi to ask the oracle why no crops grew that summer. She told him to bring back word that the land was under a curse which would only be lifted if Phrixus was sacrificed by his father.

Athamas was very sad when he heard this, but dared not disobey the oracle, which he believed was the voice of Apollo. So on the appointed day all the people gathered round the altar of Zeus on which Phrixus was to die by his father's hand.

But Nephele the Cloud Maiden would not desert her children like this. At her request kindly Pan gave her a magic ram with a fleece of pure gold; and as Athamas raised his sword to perform the sacrifice, it flew down and took Phrixus and his sister Helle on its back, and carried them away.

Over land and sea it went, bearing them in safety, but as it crossed from Europe into Asia it swooped down suddenly, and Helle tumbled off and was drowned in the narrow sea which, after her, is called Hellespont to this very day.

The ram flew on with Phrixus until it came to the land of Colchis near the world's eastern end where Aeetes the Wizard was king. There he lived in safety, and when the ram died, its Golden Fleece was hung up in a magic grove with a watchful dragon to guard it until the day when the Argonauts should come for it.

In Thebes only Ino was sorry that the two children had been saved, and punishment came to her before long.

Her next sister, the third daughter of Cadmus, was the lovely Semele; and her Zeus decided to marry himself. As her mother Harmonia had been the daughter of two Immortals, Ares and Aphrodite, he felt that their son should be a being of more than mortal powers.

Now when Hera, the Queen of Olympus, discovered

what Zeus was about, she became very angry, and her jealousy knew no bounds. She was also afraid that if Zeus and Semele had a son, he might be made an Immortal of greater power and glory than her own sons Ares and Hephaestus.

She made up her mind to destroy Semele, and the child. So one day she disguised herself as an old woman and went to call on her. She spoke kindly at first, and after a while asked who her husband was. But when Semele told her that it was Zeus himself the old woman laughed.

'Are you sure of that?' she asked. 'May it not be some ordinary mortal man who is deceiving you by pretending to be Zeus? I'm sure he does not visit you clad in the shining glory that Zeus wears on Olympus when he sits at the golden table beside his Immortal wife, Queen Hera!'

Semele was troubled by this, and next time Zeus came, she said:

'You made me a promise when we were married, that you would grant me one wish, whatever it might be.'

'I did,' answered Zeus, 'and I swear by Styx that you shall have it!'

'Then come to me in the same glory that you wear among the Immortals,' begged foolish Semele. 'Then I will know that you are Zeus indeed, and that you are not ashamed of having a mortal wife.'

Zeus sorrowed bitterly; but he could not break his oath,

though he realized that it was Hera who had tricked him like this.

He rose to his feet, raised his hand, and in a moment was transfigured with light so shining and so fierce that, being mortal, Semele could not bear it, she fell back with a shriek, and died – shrivelled up by the shining glory of Zeus.

But he took the child, whom he named Dionysus, and after caring for him for a little while, he told Hermes to look after him and guard him from Hera's jealousy.

At first Hermes entrusted him to Ino and her youngest sister Argave, telling them something of the truth, and commanding them to keep secret who he was, and for greater security to pretend that he was a girl.

So Dionysus grew safely to boyhood in Thebes, unknown to Hera. But at length he was betrayed by Ino and Argave, and Zeus only just saved him by turning him into a little goat which Hermes carried off to Mount Nysa in Thrace, where the kindly water-nymphs, daughters of the river Lamos, took care of him.

Ino was punished for this and for her earlier wickedness. She went mad and leapt into the sea, carrying her own son in her arms; but the sea-nymphs took them, and they lived ever after among the waves, and atoned for the evil which Ino had done during her life on earth, by bringing help to storm-tossed sailors.

Meanwhile Dionysus grew to manhood in the cave on

Mount Nysa, and made friends with Silenus and the Satyrs, who vowed to follow him wherever he went. For Dionysus discovered how to make wine out of the grapes which grew on Mount Nysa, and the Satyrs were the first creatures to taste this new and wonderful drink, and to grow intoxicated by it.

It was after his first drunken feast that Silenus fell asleep in the garden of King Midas, who treated him so kindly that Dionysus promised him any gift he might ask.

'Let everything I touch turn into gold!' cried greedy Midas eagerly, and Dionysus granted the wish with a merry twinkle in his eye.

Home went Midas and had very soon turned his house into gold, and his garden also with all its trees and flowers. But when he found that even food and drink turned to gold as soon as he touched them with his lips, he realized what a fool he had been, and he sought out Dionysus and begged him to take back his magic gift.

Midas did not learn wisdom by this experience, and not long afterwards he angered Apollo, who gave him ass's ears for refusing to recognize good music when he heard it.

Meanwhile Dionysus had gone out into the world to teach mankind how to grow grape-vines, and how to make the grapes into wine. He had many adventures on the way, travelling even as far as India, whence he returned in a chariot drawn by tigers. On one occasion, for example, he only escaped from his enemies by turning a river into wine, which sent them all to sleep after they had attempted to quench their thirst at it.

When at length he came to Greece, Dionysus found several kings who were anxious to prevent him from teaching their people how to make wine. The reason they gave was that, like the Satyrs, many women, who were called Maenads, followed Dionysus, and these often deserted their husbands and children to go dancing away on the lonely hillsides.

One of these kings was called Lycurgus, and he drove Dionysus into the sea, where the sea-nymphs rescued him and the loveliest of them all, Thetis, entertained him in her coral caves.

Lycurgus suffered for what he had done, since when he tried to cut down the vine which Dionysus had planted, he cut off one of his own feet instead.

Meanwhile Dionysus came up again out of the caves of Thetis, but on the wrong side of the sea, and hired a ship to carry him across. Now it chanced that the sailors were wicked pirates from Tyre who were in search of handsome young men to sell as slaves, and to them Dionysus seemed a fine prize indeed. For he was tall and shapely, with a fair skin and rich, dark hair falling upon his strong shoulders and over his cloak of deep purple.

When they were well out to sea, the Pirate Captain told his men to bind Dionysus with ropes and put him down in the dark hold of the ship. But when they tried to do so, the ropes fell again and again from his hands and feet as soon as they had been tied.

Then the helmsman cried: 'We are mad to do this! It must be one of the Immortals whom we are carrying in our ship – it may be Apollo, or Poseidon, or great Zeus himself. Let us set him free and bear him with all honour over the waves to Greece, lest he grows angry and is fearfully avenged upon us.'

The Captain was furious: 'Madman yourself!' he shouted. 'You look after your own job, and we'll attend to this fellow. He'll fetch us a fine price in Egypt or in Sidon, depend upon it!'

Then they hoisted the sails and sped away over the dancing waves with a fair wind behind them.

But soon strange things began to happen: first a sweet smell of wine rose from the hold of the ship, and a stream of it coursed across the deck. Then, while the sailors stood still in amazement, the mast and spars of the ship began to put forth leaves and long, waving tendrils. Grapes grew in great, dark bunches down either side of the sails, and the thole-pins between which the long oars rested grew up into vines clustered with flowers.

When the pirates saw all this, they cried out to the helmsman to turn the ship and steer for Greece with all the speed he could. But their remorse came too late, for even as they turned towards Dionysus to beg his mercy, he changed into a fierce lion and came bounding along the deck towards them.

With shrieks of terror, they sprang over the sides into the sea – and were changed immediately into dolphins. All except Achaetes the helmsman, who sat rooted to his seat with terror. Then Dionysus returned to his usual shape, and spoke to him kindly:

'Do not be afraid, good Achaetes, you counselled your evil companions to treat me as they should, and you have found favour in my heart. Know that I am Dionysus, son of Immortal Zeus, and that I travel to the land of Greece bearing the gift of wine to be a comfort and a joy to all mankind.'

So Achaetes steered the ship, and the winds blew it over the waves until they came to Athens. There Dionysus was kindly received and his gift was welcomed, though his host Icarius suffered a sad fate by mistake. For he offered wine to his friends and they, having drunk too much of it and feeling its strange effects for the first time, cried out that Icarius had poisoned them.

In their fear and anger they killed him and threw his body into a well, where his daughter Erigone found it with the help of his faithful dog – and hanged herself for grief. Zeus saw what had happened, and set all three among the stars, where you may see them to this day as the constellations of Virgo, Arcturus, and Procyon the Little Dog.

But Dionysus continued on his way, and came at length

to Thebes where he had been born. There no one knew him, and Pentheus, son of Argave, who was now king instead of his grandfather Cadmus, shut him up in a stone prison and swore that he would kill him.

Once again, however, the power of Dionysus triumphed. Vines grew up between the stones of the prison walls so that they fell to the ground, and Dionysus went free; while Pentheus was mistaken for a lion by a wild band of Maenads, amongst whom was his mother Argave, and they caught him and tore him to pieces.

All these and many more deeds as strange and wonderful were told of Dionysus; and men honoured him and said that he must be one of the Immortals. Yet he had one more adventure to face before he could take his seat on Olympus, and this was the strangest and one which befell no other Immortal. For he came to the land of Argos towards the south of Greece, and there King Perseus came against him fully armed and they fought.

Perseus was also a son of Zeus, and the greatest of the heroes of Greece except one, and for a little while Zeus had thought him the Hero for whom he sought.

So when Perseus drew his sword against Dionysus, all the Immortals gathered in the clouds to watch so terrible and fateful a battle. The end of it was that Perseus smote Dionysus a mortal blow: for thus only could the anger of Hera be appeased. But whether Dionysus also killed

Perseus at the same time is not known for certain, since some say that Perseus was murdered shortly afterwards by Megapenthes whose father, Proteus, he had turned to stone with the Gorgon's head.

As he died Dionysus leapt into the lake of Lerna by which they had fought: for this lake had no bottom, and led to the Realm of the Dead where Hades ruled over the souls of mortals. In this way Dionysus shared the fate of all mankind, though Zeus had decreed that he should become an Immortal and sit on Olympus.

In the Realm of Hades, Dionysus made his way to the throne where that dread king sits with pale, sad Persephone beside him.

'Lord of the dead!' cried Dionysus, 'by the will of Zeus, who is my father, I do not remain here as your subject, but rise presently through the earth and take my place with the other Immortals. But it is my desire to take my mother Semele with me: and I beg of you to release her from death so that she may accompany me.'

'That cannot be,' answered Hades in his slow, solemn tones, 'unless you give me in exchange for your mother, your best beloved who now lives upon the earth.'

'I will certainly do that,' said Dionysus, and he swore it by the River Styx, the oath which no Immortal may break.

'Good,' said Hades, and bound himself by the same oath to release Semele. 'Now for your best beloved!'

'My best beloved is here!' cried Dionysus, and he struck the thin rod, or thyrsis which he carried in his hand into the barren ground. At once it took root, sent out leaves, and grew great clusters of grapes.

'The vine is my best beloved!' he exclaimed in triumph.

Then Hades nodded his head, and Semele was given up to her son.

At the command of Zeus a chasm then opened in the earth, so deep and mysterious that no bird ever dared fly over it, and through this Dionysus passed up to Olympus, leading his mother by the hand. There the other Immortals welcomed him, and even Hera smiled and forgot her jealousy.

CHAPTER SEVEN

PERSEUS THE GORGON-SLAYER

Led by Athena I won from the grey-haired
  terrible sisters
Secrets hidden from men . . . They showed me
  the perilous pathway
Over the waterless ocean, the valley that led to
  the Gorgon.
Her too I slew in my craft, Medusa, the beautiful
  horror;
Taught by Athena I slew her, and saw not herself,
  but her image.

CHARLES KINGSLEY
Andromeda

7

Perseus was not the Hero for whom Zeus waited, though when he was born Zeus may not have been sure about it: prophecies were uncertain things, or why should he think that the Hero would be an Argive from Argolis? This was the fertile triangle of land through which the river Inachus flows down to the blue bay of Nauplia, and in it the sons of men built three fair cities, Argos, Mycenae, and Tiryns, aided by the Cyclopes, those giant servants of Zeus who had each but one eye, in the centre of the forehead. The huge stones which they raised to form the city walls may be seen, still in place, even to this day.

In Tiryns lived King Acrisius, who had one child only, a lovely girl, called Danae. Being very anxious to have a son to succeed him, Acrisius sent to ask the oracle of Apollo what he had done that this was denied him. His question was not answered; instead the oracle warned him that his daughter would have a son who would kill him.

'We'll see about that!' cried Acrisius, and, vowing that Danae should never marry, he shut her up in a tower at Tiryns which was plated all over with brass so that it shone in the sun like gold. The brass plates have gone from it today, but you can still see the brass nails embedded in the stone which once held them in place.

But Zeus visited Danae in a shower of golden rain, and spoke with her out of the shining mist, and they had a son called Perseus who was born there in the prison-tower at Tiryns.

When Acrisius heard that, in spite of all his precautions, he had a grandson, he was filled with anger and fear, and these passions made him cruel. He would not believe that Zeus was the child's father, but said that it was Proteus, his brother, whom he hated, who had stolen the key of the brazen tower and married Danae in secret.

He had a great wooden chest made, and he set Danae in it with the baby in her arms, and pushed it out on to the rippling waters in the Bay of Nauplia.

'It would be a terrible crime to kill my daughter and my grandson,' he said, 'and the Immortals would send a curse upon me. No, I am merely dispatching them across the sea – and if the waves chance to fill the chest and make it sink, I am not to blame!'

Away floated the chest over the blue sea and out of sight of land; and presently the waves began to rise and the wind to blow, and Danae wept with fear and clasped the baby Perseus close in her arms:

'Oh what a fate is yours,' she sobbed, 'and yet you do not cry but sleep as peacefully as ever, feeling no terror of the dreadful place in which we are. You do not fear the heaving sea, nor the salt spray on your hair . . . Oh, perhaps it is because you know that Father Zeus will protect us . . . Then sleep on, sweet babe, for the waves swell only to rock your cradle, and I will pray to Zeus that we may come safely to land.'

All night the chest floated over the sea, and in the morning it was washed up on the shores of the island of Seriphos where Polydectes was king. And there Dictys, the king's brother, who was a fisherman, found Danae and her child, and took them to his home and looked after them.

There Perseus grew up, a strong and noble youth skilled in all manner of things, from the craft of the fisherman to the use of the sword. In time King Polydectes heard of them, and fell in love with Danae; but she would not marry him, for he was a cruel and wicked tyrant. At length he decided to take her by force; but this he dared not do because Perseus was always there to guard her.

So he devised a scheme to remove Perseus without incurring any blame for killing him. He held a great feast to which he invited the young men of Seriphos, including Perseus, and they all came bringing rich gifts to the King.

But Perseus had nothing to give, and he alone came empty-handed, so that all the young men mocked him, until his cheeks burnt with shame.

'I'll bring a finer present than any of you!' he cried fiercely.

'That cannot be,' said cunning Polydectes, '*unless you bring me the Gorgon's Head*!'

'That I will!' shouted Perseus, 'I'll bring it, or die in the attempt!'

And with that he rushed out of the palace amid the loud laughter and jeers of Polydectes and his friends, and went down beside the quiet sea to think what he should do.

While he sat there, deep in thought, two Immortals came to him: Athena, tall and stately in her shining helmet, with her polished shield upon her arm; and Hermes with kindly laughter in his eyes, slim and quick of limb, with the winged sandals on his feet.

'Do not grieve, Perseus,' said Hermes, 'for, by the will of Zeus, we are come to help you. See, here I lend you the sharpest weapon in the world, that very sickle of adamant with which Cronos wounded the Sky, and which

Zeus used in his battle with Typhon. No lesser blade will smite the head from Medusa the Gorgon.'

'And I,' said Athena in her calm, sweet voice, 'will lend you my shield with which I dazzle the eyes of erring mortals who do battle against my wisdom. Any mortal who looks upon the face of Medusa is turned to stone immediately by the terror of it: but if you look only on her reflection in the shield, all will be well.'

'Rise now,' said Hermes, 'your mother will be safe until your return, for the good fisherman, Dictys, will protect her – and you have far to travel. First you must visit the Grey Sisters and learn from them how to find the Nymphs who dwell at the back of the North Wind: they will lend you all else that you may need, and will tell you how to find the Gorgons, and how to escape from the two who are immortal, when you have slain Medusa.'

So Perseus hastened away, his heart beating with excitement at the thought of the high adventure which was his, and the great honour which the Immortals had done him.

He came, as Hermes had instructed him, to the lonely cave in the dark north where the three daughters of the Titan Phorcus lived, the Grey Sisters who had been born old women with grey hair, and who had only one eye and one tooth between them.

Perseus stepped quietly up behind them as they sat near the mouth of their cave; and as they passed the single eye from one to another, he took it from an outstretched hand, and then cried aloud:

'Daughters of Phorcus, I have your eye! And I will keep it and leave you for ever in darkness if you do not tell me what I wish to know.'

The Grey Sisters cried aloud in alarm: 'Give us back our eye, and we will swear by Styx to tell you truthfully all you ask. But do not leave us for ever in this terrible darkness!'

So Perseus learnt the way to the magic land at the back of the North Wind and, returning the eye, hastened on his journey.

When he reached the lovely garden of the Northern Nymphs, he was welcomed kindly by them, and he rested for a long time in the paradise where they dwelt for ever young and happy.

But at length he said: 'Fair Nymphs, I must hasten away to kill the Gorgon Medusa and carry her head to wicked King Polydectes. Tell me, I beg of you, where the Gorgons live, and how I may kill Medusa.'

'We will lend you the Shoes of Swiftness,' answered the Nymphs, 'so that you may escape from Medusa's terrible sisters. And we will lend you this magic wallet in which to carry away the head. There is but one thing wanting, and that is the Cap of Hades, the dog-skin cap which makes its wearer invisible.'

Then one of the Nymphs went swiftly down to the Realm of Hades, for she had been Persephone's favourite companion on earth, and could visit the Queen of the Dead whenever she wished, and returned at will.

She brought back the Cap of Darkness, so that Perseus now had all things needful, and was ready for his dreadful task.

He bade farewell to the kind Nymphs, and set out on the way which the Grey Sisters had told him, and he came at last to the stony land of the Gorgons. As he drew near to where they lived, he saw all about in the fields and on the roads, the statues of men and beasts which had been living creatures until turned to stone by the deadly glance of the Gorgons.

Then he saw the three terrible sisters lying asleep in the sun with the snakes which grew instead of hair writhing about the head of Medusa, and the dragon-scales which covered her sisters' heads. They had white tusks like pigs and hands of brass; and great golden wings grew from their shoulders.

Wearing the Cap of Darkness, and stepping cautiously, Perseus drew near, looking only at the reflection in Athena's polished shield. Then he trembled indeed as he saw the terrible face of Medusa pictured on the bright surface; but he did not draw back. Still looking only at the reflection, he drew the adamantine sickle and cut off the terrible head at a single blow. Then, quick as could be, he picked it up and dropped it into the wallet which the Nymphs had given him.

But the hissing of the snakes on Medusa's head woke the other two Gorgons, who could not be killed, and they sprang up, eager to avenge their sister.

Perseus leapt into the air and sped away on the Shoes of Swiftness as fast as he could go. After him came the Gorgons, screaming with rage, but Perseus fled away and away out over the dark ocean, south, ever south until his terrible pursuers were lost in the distance behind him.

Then Perseus turned east and flew over Africa, across the great empty desert where there was no green thing, and no drop of water. As he went the blood soaked through the magic wallet and dripped behind him, and wherever a drop touched the thirsty sand, it became a green oasis.

Night came, and in the morning as he flew over the sea-shore he beheld what at first he thought was a wonderful statue of a fair girl hewn from the rock just above sea-level.

Swooping down, Perseus found that it was no statue but a living maiden chained naked to the face of the rock, with the little waves creeping up to her feet.

'Chained maiden!' said Perseus gently. 'My heart bleeds for you!'

'Who speaks? Who is it pities poor doomed Andromeda?' she cried wildly.

Perseus had forgotten that he still wore the Cap of Invisibility. Now he removed it swiftly, and hovering above the waves he said:

'Lovely Andromeda, why are you chained here?'

Then, weeping bitterly, she told him how her foolish mother, Cassiopea, had offended the sea-nymphs by her ridiculous boastings, and they had sent a monster to ravage all the sea coast, until King Cepheus, her father, chained her there as a sacrifice, hoping thus to satisfy the creature's fury.

'If I can save you, will you at least remember me?' asked Perseus, who had fallen in love with Andromeda at first sight.

'Do not make me weep, dreaming of deeds that can never be done!' she sobbed.

'Deeds that men deemed impossible have been accomplished, none the less,' he answered. Then he turned quickly away, for he had noticed a ripple in the sea drawing nearer, ever nearer. Perseus, still hovering just above the waves, got ready; and in a few moments the monster raised its head above the water and opened wide its fierce jaws. Then, while Andromeda screamed, and her parents on the cliffs above wept and prayed, Perseus drew the Gorgon's head from his wallet and held it in front of the savage eyes. And the monster sank back, still and cold and silent, a long ridge of jagged stone.

Then Perseus returned the head to the magic wallet, cut Andromeda's chains with the adamantine sickle, and carried her in safety to the cliff top.

There was great rejoicing at the rescue of Andromeda,

and King Cepheus readily agreed that Perseus should marry her. So there Perseus stayed for many days, and there was a noble feast at his wedding. But as they sat at the great table, the door was flung suddenly open, and a great man strode in followed by a band of desperadoes all armed with drawn swords:

'Yield up Andromeda to me!' shouted the leader of this band, who was a prince named Phineus. 'She was promised to me, and unless I get her, I'll slaughter every man here, burn the city and carry off the women to be my slaves!'

Then Perseus strode down the hall until he stood in front of Phineus, and taking out the Gorgon's head he turned him and all his followers to stone on the instant.

Not long after this, Perseus and Andromeda set sail for Greece and came at length to the island of Seriphos. Here he found that his mother Danae had been made a slave by Polydectes, while Dictys his kind friend languished in prison.

Leaving Andromeda on the ship, Perseus went alone up to the palace and found Polydectes sitting at meat with the same band of followers who had jeered at him once before.

'Well, if it isn't that landless boaster, Perseus!' cried the king scornfully, while the others laughed and jested at him. 'Have you, by any chance, brought me the present you promised?'

'Yes,' answered Perseus quietly. 'I come, according to my promise, bringing the Gorgon's head.'

'Boaster and liar!' jeered Polydectes. 'Do you think to frighten us with empty words? Show us this wonder – if you can.'

Perseus answered nothing, but pulled the Gorgon's head out of the wallet and held it up for all to see. And afterwards the stone lumps which had once been men were dragged out and dumped on the hillside.

That evening Hermes came to Perseus and received back from him the Sickle and the Shield and with them the Cap, the Shoes, and the Wallet. He also took the head of Medusa, which Athena set in the centre of her shield to strike terror into the hearts of the Giants when the long-expected invasion should take place.

After this Dictys became King of Seriphos, and married Danae, while Perseus and Andromeda set sail for Argolis. But on the way he stopped at Larissa and took part in the great games which the king of that land was holding.

Perseus distinguished himself greatly in these; but when it came to throwing the round iron disc, he hurled it so hard that it struck an old man who sat watching, and killed him instantly. This, it turned out, was Acrisius, who had left Tiryns in fear that Perseus, on his return, would kill him and so fulfil the oracle.

Sorrowing deeply, Perseus went on his way; and he and Andromeda ruled over Argolis for many years and had numerous children. Among these were Electryon and Alcaeus. The first of these became the father of Alcmena and the second was the father of Amphitryon; and these two cousins married, and went to live in Thebes. And there was a third son called Sthenelus, who late in life had a son called Eurystheus, who ruled over Tiryns and all Argos.

Perseus perished after his battle with Dionysus, and Zeus set him among the stars, with Andromeda beside him: but the son of his granddaughter Alcmena was destined to be the Hero who was to surpass all others in strength and mighty deeds, and who was to help Zeus in his war with the Giants. For this child was Heracles, whom the Romans called Hercules.

CHAPTER EIGHT

THE BIRTH OF HERACLES

The lay records the labours, and the praise,
And all the immortal acts of Hercules.
First, how the mighty babe, when swathed in
  bands,
The serpents strangled with his infant hands.

VIRGIL
Aeneid (Translated by John Dryden)

8

Electryon, the son of Perseus, had an only daughter called Alcmena, whom he promised in marriage to his nephew Amphitryon. All his sons were killed while fighting a band of robbers who had stolen his great herd of cattle, and Amphitryon was to marry Alcmena and become king of all Argolis when the cattle were recovered and the dead princes revenged.

Amphitryon began by repurchasing the stolen cattle for a large sum of money, which he suggested that Electryon should pay.

'I'll pay no money to regain my own cattle!' shouted

Electryon. 'If you've been fool enough to buy back stolen property, you yourself must suffer the consequences of your folly.'

In a moment of temper at this rebuff Amphitryon flung away the club with which he had been driving the cattle, and by an evil chance it struck a horn of one of the cows, rebounded, and killed Electryon.

After this, Sthenelus, youngest son of Perseus, banished his nephew Amphitryon from Argolis on a charge of murder, and ruled in his place.

Amphitryon fled to Thebes, and Alcmena went with him:

'I know you only killed my father by accident,' she said, 'so I will still marry you: but on one condition. You must first punish the robbers who killed my brothers.'

At Thebes, King Creon was now ruler. He had come to the throne after the banishment of the famous King Oedipus who saved Thebes from the terrible Sphinx. The Sphinx was a monster, with a lion's body, eagle's wings, and a woman's head; she sat on a great rock near the city and asked everyone who passed to answer a riddle. And what she asked was this:

'What creature, with only one voice, has four legs in the morning, two at midday and three in the evening; and yet is weakest when it has most?'

All who failed to answer the riddle, she ate immediately, and no one found the correct answer until young Oedipus came to Thebes. He replied: 'The creature is a man. For as a child, in the morning of his days, he goes on all fours and yet is weakest. In the middle of his life he walks upon his two legs, and is strongest; but in old age he needs the aid of a stick, and so three legs support him.'

At this the Sphinx screamed with fury, and cast herself down from the rock and was killed. Then Oedipus ruled well and wisely at Thebes, until a curse fell upon the land because of crimes which he had committed unintentionally, and he wandered away as a blind beggar, leaving his uncle Creon as king.

When Amphitryon came to Thebes he found that another curse had descended on that unlucky city. For the Teumessian Fox, which was as large and savage as a wolf, had been sent by Dionysus to plague the land, catching children and carrying them away to its lair, as a punishment for the things he had suffered in Thebes.

Now this was an enchanted fox which nobody could catch, for it ran faster than the fastest creature in the world.

'If you can rid us of this fox,' said Creon, 'I will lend you an army to take vengeance on the robbers.'

Amphitryon agreed to this, for he knew of a magic hound which was fated to catch whatever it pursued. With the help of Artemis, he was able to borrow this dog, and he set it upon the trail of the fox. The uncatchable was being chased by the inescapable; but Zeus saw what was happening, and made haste to turn both fox and dog into stone. Then Amphitryon set out to punish the robbers (with the aid of Creon's men) and Alcmena got ready to marry him the moment he returned victorious.

But the time was growing short now. Already the Giants were stirring under the dark northern hills, and still the Hero was not born who was to save both men and Immortals. Zeus looked about him anxiously, and on a sudden realized that the time had come. For the Hero, he believed, was to be born in Thebes – and was also to be a member of the royal family of Argolis, descended from Danae whom he had visited in the shower of gold.

Alcmena, the granddaughter of Perseus, dwelt at Thebes, waiting but for the return of Amphitryon to be her husband: surely here indeed was the mother of the Hero?

Alcmena was the loveliest woman alive at that time, though her beauty could not compare with that of Helen, who would be born not many years later. She was taller than other women, wiser and more noble. Her face and her dark eyes seemed like those of Immortal Aphrodite herself; she was good and virtuous, one who would always be true to Amphitryon.

This being so, how was Zeus to marry Alcmena? For long he pondered, and a pang of regret passed through his heart as he thought how he must cheat her. Yet it had to be done, for the Hero must be born, to free mankind from many evils, and the Immortals from the unconquerable Giants.

While Zeus pondered, Amphitryon overcame the robbers, punished them thoroughly for what they had done, and set out rejoicing for Thebes, having sent a messenger before him to bid Alcmena make ready for the wedding.

Then Zeus came down swiftly from Olympus, and by his powers put on the very shape and voice and likeness of Amphitryon. He arrived at Thebes, dusty from travel, and Alcmena welcomed him without any shadow of suspicion, and the wedding was celebrated that very evening.

That night was the longest the world has known, for by command of Zeus the Sun-Titan, Helios, did not drive forth his flaming chariot next day, and Hermes visited the Silver Lady, Selene, begging her to linger in her course across the sky with the pale Moon in her cloud-washed boat. Kindly Sleep leant his aid also, making mankind so drowsy and sending them such sweet dreams that no one suspected that this one night was the length of three.

Whether Amphitryon was overtaken by sleep or not, he failed to reach Thebes until the rosy-fingered Morning was awake in the east – Eos, who harnesses the golden horses to the chariot of the Sun. He came straight to Alcmena, but maybe Zeus met him on the way and told him of what had chanced: for it was long before she knew that she was doubly wedded on that triple night.

The months passed, and the time drew near when the child was to be born, and Zeus, certain that he would be the Hero destined to save the Immortals, could not contain his satisfaction.

'Today,' he told the other Immortals as they sat on their golden thrones on Olympus, drinking nectar and eating ambrosia – the wine and food, made only in heaven, which keeps those who partake of it for ever young and fair to look on. 'Today,' repeated Zeus with a sigh of pleasure, 'there will be born a boy, a descendant of Perseus, who will be lord over all the people of Argolis.'

He would have said more, but jealous Hera interrupted quickly, saying:

'Of Argolis? Of the land which is my special care? Well, so be it! But swear an oath now that what you have said will surely happen.'

Surprised, but anxious to please her, Zeus swore the unbreakable oath by Styx, the Black River of Hades, and changed the subject quickly.

Hera hastened in triumph to Argos, accompanied by her daughter Eilithyia who presides over the birth of children. By witchcraft she made sure that Heracles was not born until *next day*, but that his cousin Eurystheus, the son of King Sthenelus, was born instead, much earlier than was expected.

While these things were happening on earth, Zeus sat happily on Olympus chatting with Ate, another daughter whom Hera had instructed to keep him occupied while she and Eilithyia were busy in Argolis and Thebes.

When she returned to Olympus she cried in triumph:

'Now your promise is performed, great Zeus, for Eurystheus, grandson of Perseus, has just been born at Tiryns – and today is ended!'

In his fury, Zeus seized Ate by the hair and flung her out of heaven:

'Go and wander over the earth!' he cried, 'and stir up trouble among men! Wherever you go there shall be wars and troubles, caused by you!'

Ate landed in Phrygia, near the city of Troy, which became the scene of the greatest war in all the history of ancient Greece.

But Zeus could not break his oath, so it came about that Heracles became the slave of Eurystheus in after years.

In the meantime, he was born a day late in Thebes, and with him a twin brother, the son of Amphitryon, who was named Iphicles, and who came into the world an hour later than Heracles – but very far indeed behind him in courage.

When they were no more than ten months old, Heracles performed his first feat of valour.

It happened on a summer's evening when Alcmena had bathed the two babies, given them their milk and rocked them to sleep in a cradle made out of a big bronze shield which Amphitryon had brought back as a prize from his campaign against the robbers.

'Sleep, my little ones!' crooned Alcmena. 'Sleep softly, and pass safely through the dark night and into the gentle morning, my twin babes!'

Darkness fell, and all the house grew still. But at the hour of midnight Hera sent two monstrous snakes with scales of azure blue, to slay the infant Heracles. Writhing and curling along the ground they came, shining with a strange, baleful light, and spitting deadly venom.

But when they drew near the children (for all the doors flew open before them), Zeus caused the babes to wake. Iphicles, seeing the serpents curling up to strike with their cruel fangs, screamed with fright, and kicking off his coverlet rolled out on to the floor.

Heracles, however, sat up smiling in the brazen shield, and grasped a snake in either hand, gripping them by their necks and keeping the poisoned fangs well away from him. The serpents hissed horribly, and twined their cruel coils about the child. But Heracles held on, squeezing and squeezing with his tiny hands, trying to throttle them with his strong little fingers.

Then Alcmena heard the screams of Iphicles and, running to the room, saw the unearthly light flickering through the open door which she had closed so carefully.

'Arise, Amphitryon!' she cried. 'Do you not hear how loud our younger child is wailing? Do you not see the light flickering on the walls? Surely some terrible creature has come into the house!'

Amphitryon sprang up, seized his sword, and rushed into the nursery, with Alcmena close behind him carrying a lamp.

There they found Heracles grasping a dead snake in either hand, shaking them fiercely, and crowing with delight. But Iphicles lay on the floor, his eyes wide with terror, too scared even to cry any more.

Proudly the baby Heracles showed the serpents to Amphitryon and Alcmena, then flinging them from him, snuggled down once more and went quietly to sleep.

In the morning Alcmena, feeling that there must be something strange about her child Heracles, went to consult the ancient prophet Tiresias, the wisest man in Thebes.

Strange things were told of Tiresias, who was blind, and who had already lived three times as long as any ordinary man. It was said that when he was a boy two enchanted snakes turned him into a woman, and that a year later they made him a man again. And that once, when Zeus and Hera had an argument, Hera saying that Zeus had a much better time than she did, they had consulted Tiresias, who replied that it was nine times as pleasant to be a woman as to be a man.

Hera was furious at this, and struck Tiresias blind in that instant. Zeus could not undo what another Immortal had done, but he gave Tiresias the gift of prophecy and decreed that he should live for more than three generations.

'Tell me what all this means,' Alcmena begged Tiresias, when she had related the adventure with the serpents. 'It is not natural that a child of ten months should do all that Heracles has done. So tell me the truth, I beg, even if you see much suffering and sorrow in the future for me and mine.'

'Be of good cheer, granddaughter of Perseus,' answered the old prophet solemnly, 'for your son is destined to be the most famous mortal who ever trod the soil of Greece. He shall rid the land of monsters, and do many labours of which poets will tell in song and story for ever. Many things shall he suffer also and the long enmity of Hera, Queen of the Immortals, who sent those serpents against him. But in the end he shall stand beside the Immortals in their direst need, and afterwards shall become one of them and sit on Olympus for ever. For know that he is the Hero, the son of Zeus, whose coming was foretold at the beginning of the world by Prometheus, the good Titan.'

Then Tiresias went on to tell Alcmena what had happened on her wedding-night, and how she was in reality the bride of Zeus, and the most honoured among mortal women, to be the mother of Heracles.

After this Heracles grew quickly and in safety, well tended by Alcmena and her husband, who was not in the least jealous of Zeus.

At first Heracles learnt all the gentle arts: how to sing, how to play sweetly on the lyre and how to read and write. Then Amphitryon taught him how to drive a chariot skilfully; and he learnt also the use of sword and spear, and the whole art of boxing and wrestling. None could throw a dart more truly than Heracles, and of all archers he was the best, sending an arrow further than any other mortal, more swiftly, and with deadly aim.

It was plain to see, even when he was young, that Heracles was the son of an Immortal. For he was a head taller than any other man, and broad in proportion, while his eyes flashed fire.

But his temper was very violent, and when he was still only a boy he killed Linus who was teaching him to play the lyre. For Linus struck him angrily one day when he played a false note, and Heracles struck back so violently with the instrument which he held in his hand that Linus fell dead immediately.

Heracles was pardoned for this deed; but Amphitryon, fearing lest some such mischance might happen again, sent him away from Thebes, to tend the cattle on Mount Cithaeron. And here Heracles increased in strength and skill; and at last he drew near to manhood.

CHAPTER NINE

THE CHOICE OF HERACLES

First, then, he made the wood
Of Zeus a solitude,
Slaying its lion-tenant; and he spread
The tawniness behind – his yellow head
Enmuffled by the brute's, backed by that grin of
  dread.

EURIPIDES
Heracles (Translated by Robert Browning)

9

While Heracles was guarding the cattle of Amphitryon on the lonely slopes of Mount Cithaeron,
and still ignorant of his high destiny, a strange thing befell
him.

As he sat alone on the hillside one day, wondering if
he was fated to be a cow-herd all his life, or whether it
would not be better to become a wild robber of the mountains, he saw two lovely maidens coming towards him.
One of them was dressed in simple white, and had modest,
down-cast eyes and a calm, gentle face from which seemed
to shine both goodness and wisdom; but the other wore

bright colours, and came striding along glancing boldly about her – now admiring herself, and now looking to others for admiration. She was decked with rich jewels, and her face was artfully touched with paint and with powder.

As they drew near to Heracles, the second, as if anxious to forestall her companion, pushed eagerly ahead and spoke to him:

'Dear Heracles,' she said, 'I see that you have reached the age when you must choose what kind of life yours is to be. So I have come to urge you to take me as your friend and let me guide you on your way. I promise that if you do I will lead you by the easiest and most delightful paths. You shall taste every pleasure, and no troubles or toils shall come near you. Your life shall be passed in the pursuit and enjoyment of pleasant things, with no labour of body or mind, except to please yourself without any thought for the cares of others.'

She paused, and Heracles asked: 'Lady, tell me your name.'

Then she answered softly: 'Heracles, those who love me call me Happiness, but my enemies, it is true, have another name which I do not care to mention.'

Meanwhile the modest maiden had come up, and now she spoke:

'I too, noble Heracles, am come to offer you a way of life. I know of what a worthy line you come, that you are descended from Perseus the Gorgon-slayer, and are yourself the son of Zeus. I know how well you have learnt all the accomplishments necessary for the path which I trust that you will take, in my company. Follow me, and you will do great deeds and leave a name which will never be forgotten. But you cannot win what is glorious and excellent in the world without care and labour: the gods give no real good, no true happiness to men on earth on any other terms. If you would bring happiness to others and be remembered in Greece, you must strive for the service of Greece – as you well may with your strength and your skill, if you do but use them rightly. As for my companion, who is called Vice and Folly and other such names, do not be misled by her: there is no pleasure and no happiness like those which you earn by strife and labour and with the sweat of your brow.'

'Do not believe this foolish girl, who is called Virtue!' interrupted Vice hastily. '*My* way to happiness is short and pleasant; hers is hard, and long, and the end is doubtful.'

'Come, Heracles,' said Virtue quietly, 'choose which of us you will follow. Her path leads through easy, worthless pleasures that grow stale and horrible and yet are craved after more and more. But follow me through toil and suffering to the great heritage which Zeus has planned for you.'

'Lady!' cried Heracles, 'I choose your path! Tell me how

to set my foot on it, and I will not turn back however hard it prove, and whatever I have to endure on the way.'

'You have chosen worthily,' she said in her calm, gentle voice. 'And for the beginning – look yonder! What is it that disturbs your cattle so?'

Heracles looked across the valley, and saw a great yellow lion leaping down the slope with open jaws towards the cows, who fled this way and that, lowing piteously in terror.

With a shout of fury Heracles sprang to his feet and went charging down the valley and up the other side. But by the time he got there, the lion had gone, and one of the cows lay dead.

'I'll kill that lion, or perish in the attempt!' cried Heracles angrily, and he turned back towards the two strange maidens – but there was no one to be seen.

Heracles returned to Thebes for his brother Iphicles, who took charge of the cattle, and he himself set out to trail the lion to its den. He did not succeed in this, however, and after a night and a day on Cithaeron he came down into a distant valley where dwelt King Thestius with his fifty beautiful daughters.

He was welcomed at the palace, and there he stayed for fifty nights, entertained kindly by the fifty lovely princesses who took it in turns to attend upon the young man, who spent each day hunting upon the mountain.

After fifty days Heracles at length tracked the great lion

to its lair, a cave in a dark, evil-smelling crevice of the rocks. Armed with a great club of olive wood cut roughly from a tree which he had torn up by the roots, Heracles strode boldly into the cave.

The great yellow lion came at him, roaring horribly, and Heracles retreated so as to have more light. In the entrance to the cave he stood at bay, and as the lion leapt, he struck it on the head with the club, bringing it to the ground, where it stood, trembling all over while its head swayed from side to side from the force of the blow.

Heracles struck once more, and the great beast lay dead before him. Then he pulled a knife from his belt and tried to skin it, but the hide was too tough. In vain he sharpened the knife on a stone, and even tried with the stone itself. It was only when he had cut out one of the terrible claws that he had an instrument keen enough for his task.

When the skin was off, Heracles dried and cured it carefully, and wore it ever afterwards tied over his shoulders and round his waist, with the scalp over his head like a helmet, so that it served both as clothing and armour.

On his way back to Thebes, Heracles met with a messenger from a certain King Eriginus, who was on his way to collect tribute from the Thebans whom he had conquered in war some years before this and robbed of all their weapons and armour.

Heracles was furious when he heard what the messenger wanted, and insulted him so grossly in his rage that King

Eriginus sent a band of armed men to Thebes demanding that Heracles should be given up to him for punishment. Creon, King of Thebes, was ready to do this, for the Thebans had nothing with which to fight.

Heracles however gathered together the young men and armed them with the sacred trophies which hung in the temple of Athena. He taught them quickly how to use these weapons, and then led them against the company of men sent by King Eriginus, whom they defeated and drove out of Thebes.

Full of rage, Eriginus gathered an army and set out to destroy the city, but Heracles ambushed them in a narrow mountain pass and defeated them almost single-handed, killing the king and most of his captains. A quick march over the hills with his band of Theban youths gave Eriginus's little city into their hands, and the inhabitants were themselves forced to bring tribute each year to Thebes.

Amphitryon was killed in the battle, but Alcmena found a good second husband at Thebes, and lived there quietly for the rest of her life.

King Creon was so grateful for what Heracles had done – and so afraid lest he might think of seeking revenge for his willingness to give him up to Eriginus, that he made haste to offer him his daughter Megara in marriage.

The wedding was celebrated with great rejoicings, and Heracles settled down with every hope of becoming king of Thebes when Creon died.

So several years passed, and Heracles had three sons whom he adored, and for whose future he planned great things.

Now, living quietly in Thebes, Heracles did no great deeds of valour, nor did he free Greece from any plagues; and Zeus was troubled, seeing that the Hero was not fitting himself for his great task.

Hera was troubled also, though for a very different reason.

'What of your oath?' she cried to Zeus one day. 'You swore that Eurystheus of Argolis should rule over all the natives of that land, and yet Heracles the greatest of them dwells safely in Thebes, and will soon become king of the city which Cadmus built.'

Then Zeus answered: 'Hera, Queen of Olympus, do not be jealous any longer. Fate holds many troubles in store for Heracles, but what good will it do if he lives merely as a captain in Argolis, second only to Eurystheus?'

'I would have him as slave to Eurystheus!' cried Hera viciously.

'That I will grant,' answered Zeus. 'Let him serve that cowardly lord of Argolis, performing ten labours for him, the hardest that can be devised, and if he survives them, then grant him his freedom.'

'I agree to that,' said Hera, 'for I will help Eurystheus to choose the tasks which Heracles must perform. But how shall we contrive to bring this servitude about? Force is useless against him, and if Eurystheus tries to make him his slave, Heracles will certainly kill him, come what may.'

Zeus sighed; then he answered sadly:

'Hera, my Queen, it shall be as you wish. Send madness upon Heracles so that, unknowing what he does, he may commit murder and be driven as an exile from Thebes. Go, see to it!'

Zeus nodded his head, and as Olympus shook to confirm his words, Hera sped gleefully on her way. But at a word from Zeus, Athena followed quietly to help Heracles as far as possible.

Now that morning the sons of Heracles and their cousins, the children of Iphicles, were engaged in martial exercises on the plain of Thebes, with other boys and young men of the city.

Heracles sat on a hillside watching them, his bow on his back and a quiver full of arrows by his side. Suddenly a dark shadow crossed the sun, and a low, evil moaning drew near and seemed to pause above his head. Then Heracles staggered to his feet, his eyes rolling wildly and foam starting from his lips.

'Enemies are upon us!' he cried. 'Eurystheus of Argolis comes to take us prisoners and make us his slaves! I will not suffer it! Alone I will save Thebes and protect my beloved children from servitude!'

In his madness, he fitted an arrow to his bow, aimed

and loosed it with such skill that his eldest son sank dead upon the plain. Then, while the boys fled away shrieking with terror, he sent arrow after arrow screaming after them, until all three of his sons lay dead, with two of Iphicles' as well.

He would have done worse deeds, but Athena came at this moment, and seeing how quickly and how fatally the madness had worked, she took up a great stone and cast it at Heracles, laying him stunned and insensible on the ground. In this state he was bound and carried to Thebes where, Creon being too old to interfere, Lycus, a pretender to the throne, declared himself king and Heracles banished for murder.

When the madness had left him Heracles in his misery and despair shut himself up in a dark room and refused to see or speak to anybody. No one dared to come near, until at length King Thestius visited him by command of Zeus, and told him that he must go to Delphi and ask Apollo how he was to atone for the terrible things he had done.

Then Heracles roused himself, gathered the lion skin about his shoulders, took the club in his hand and departed from Thebes for ever: for now his children were dead, and his wife Megara had died of a broken heart.

When he came to Delphi, the voice of the oracle spoke to him out of the dark chasm beneath the temple:

'Heracles, son of Zeus, the time has come for you to

begin the labours which will make you famous ever more, and which will fit you for the great purpose for which you were born. Go now to Eurystheus, who rules over Argolis, in his high citadel of Tiryns, and serve him faithfully in the tasks which he shall set you, doing him no harm nor striving to wrest the kingdom from him. At the last it may be that Zeus will raise you to Olympus and give you a place among the Immortals.'

So Heracles set out for Argolis, accompanied only by his nephew Iolaus, the son of Iphicles, who refused to desert him.

CHAPTER TEN

THE BEGINNING OF THE LABOURS

Are ye the same that in your strength of yore
Strangled the Nemean lion, from whose roar
The herdsmen fled as by the Alastor crossed;
Smote Lerna's Hydra, smote the Centaur host . . .
The boar on Erymanthus: and in Hell
The Hound Echidna-born, untamable . . .
All these and other Labours have I won.

SOPHOCLES
Trachiniai (Translated by Gilbert Murray)

10

Eurystheus, the cowardly weakling who had become King of Argolis after Amphitryon was banished, lived in the mighty fortress of Tiryns, whose great walls had been built by the Cyclopes, and whose narrow gateway led beneath the Brazen Tower in which Acrisius had kept Danae prisoner.

He was delighted when Heracles arrived and gave him Apollo's message.

'Well, you're a fine great hulking fellow!' he cried insolently. 'Be sure that I'll work you hard, though I doubt whether you'll be able to perform any of the Labours which I have in store for you. As a beginning, off you go up the valley and over the hills towards Corinth. Halfway there, turn left into the mountains, and bring me back the dead body of the Nemean Lion.'

Now this Lion had fallen from the moon, and was ravaging the lands all round Nemea. Nobody could kill it, for it was invulnerable, its hide so hard that neither iron nor bronze nor stone could pierce it.

Heracles set out, and near Nemea he met a shepherd who told him which way to go.

'But you've no hope of killing that Lion,' the shepherd warned him. 'He has ravaged the land all about his lair, and nobody dares to go near him. Still, I'll make a sacrifice to Zeus, and perhaps he will at least give you an easy death.'

'Wait thirty days,' said Heracles shortly, 'and if I have not returned by then, offer your sacrifice – but not to Zeus – to me, as a dead Hero!' Then he went on his way, armed with his club, his bow, a quiver full of sharp-tipped arrows, and a great sword by his side.

For a long while he searched in vain, but at last one evening he discovered the den of the fearsome Lion, which had two entrances and was strewn with the bones of men and cattle.

Heracles waited near by, and presently the great tawny beast came prowling up the hillside, its mane streaked with the blood of its latest kill and its tongue licking the great bearded chin.

Setting an arrow to the string, Heracles drew it to his ear and loosed. The swift shaft hummed to its mark, but the sharp point rebounded from the Lion's flank and fell harmlessly to the ground.

With a cry of rage, Heracles drew his sword and charged, lunging with all his strength at the Lion's chest as the huge creature reared up on its hind legs to strike at him with its mighty claws. But the tempered iron bent as if it had been lead, and the Lion, though it fell backwards, then crouched for a spring, roaring horribly.

Suddenly Heracles remembered the lion which he had slain on Cithaeron, and taking his club in both hands he dealt this one a smashing blow on the head. The Lion stood dazed for a moment, then fled to its lair, where it turned, snarling, to wait for its adversary.

Realizing that no weapon could kill it, Heracles rushed into the cave with his cloak wrapped round one arm, and seized the Lion round the neck with the other. Then they rolled and wrestled on the ground, over and over, the Lion's struggles growing ever weaker and weaker, until at last it lay dead, throttled by the mighty arm about its neck. Before it died it made one final effort and bit off one of Heracles's fingers.

When the beast was dead, and he had rested and recovered from the battle, Heracles flung the body across his shoulders and strode off towards Tiryns. On the way he found the shepherd getting ready the sacrifice, which he was quite certain would need to be offered to the ghost of the dead hero.

Heracles laughed when he saw what was happening. 'I'll join you in your prayers,' he cried jovially, 'but we'll make them to great Zeus, the giver of victory. You cannot sacrifice to a living man!'

Then he returned to Tiryns, and flung down the grizzly carcass before Eurystheus, who squeaked with horror and indignation.

'Take the nasty thing away!' he commanded, 'and never dare to come into the city again, if you return from any more Labours. But the next one will not be accomplished so easily. Go and kill the Lernean Hydra!'

The Second Labour was much more dangerous and difficult than the first, for the Hydra was a great serpent, with nine heads, which lived in the marshes of Lerna not far from Argos. It was so venomous that its very breath was deadly and it was the terror of the whole district.

Accompanied by Iolaus, Heracles drove down to the edge of the marsh in his chariot, and there Athena appeared to him.

'When you draw near to the Hydra's lair,' she said, 'you must make it come out by shooting fiery arrows into the cave. But when you fight, take care to hold your breath, for its very smell is deadly. Remember also that the centre head is immortal!'

Heracles thanked Athena, and did as she advised. After

crossing the marsh and reaching the hillock of firm ground on which the Hydra lived, Heracles bade Iolaus light a fire, and then, tying blazing bundles of grass to his arrows, he shot them into the cave.

Out came the Hydra, hissing fiercely; and holding his breath, Heracles leapt forward and shattered the nearest head with a blow of his club. But what was his horror and consternation when, from the bleeding neck sprang out two new heads, each as fierce and deadly as the old! To make matters worse, a gigantic crab came scuttling out of the marsh and grabbed Heracles by the foot.

With a roar of rage, he crushed the crab with a single blow of his club, and shouted to Iolaus to light a torch and come to his assistance. Iolaus obeyed bravely, and as Heracles crushed each head of the Hydra with his club, he burnt and seared the shattered neck so that no new heads could grow from the bleeding stumps.

When at last the battle was over, Heracles cut off the immortal head with his sword and buried it under a gigantic rock, where doubtless it lies safely to this day. Then, having dipped his arrows in the Hydra's blood, thus making them deadly poisonous, he returned to his task-master.

'You have cheated!' cried Eurystheus, when he heard all the story. 'Iolaus helped you, and your Labours must be performed by you alone. This one does not count, so you have still nine to accomplish. Off you go now, and for the next one bring me the Hind with the Golden Horns!'

This creature was a wonderful reindeer, sacred to Artemis, who had once seen five of them away in the distant north and capturing four by her fleetness of foot tamed them and harnessed them to her chariot. The fifth Hind wandered free in the hills of Arcadia, by the lovely river Cerynites, and no one dared touch it, knowing that it belonged to Artemis.

Heracles did not wish to harm this lovely creature and, though it was the swiftest of all deer, he chased it on foot for a whole year. On this quest he journeyed to the land at the back of the north wind, wandered there in the great, sweet-smelling pine forests, and came back into Greece, still pursuing the Hind. At length he overtook it in Arcadia, as it drew near to its usual dwelling-place.

As he was bringing it towards Tiryns, Artemis, the Immortal Huntress, met him in anger and cried:

'Rash mortal, how dare you seize and carry away my Hind? Surely there is no reason why I should not immediately slay you with one of my golden arrows?'

Then Heracles answered humbly, telling her that it was not of his own will but at the command of Eurystheus that he was carrying the Cerynitian Hind to Tiryns. Artemis smiled when she heard the story of his quest, and her anger departed from her.

'Go on and show my Hind to your master,' she said,

'but be sure that you do it no harm, and that you return it to my sacred grove on the hills above the Cerynitian river – otherwise Eurystheus will feel my anger!'

Heracles delivered her message faithfully, and Eurystheus lived in terror until the Hind with the Golden Horns had been returned to its Immortal owner.

'Now,' he said, with a sigh of relief when this was done, 'bring me the Erymanthian Boar, and bring it alive, in case Apollo makes any fuss about it, as I believe it has something to do with him.'

This Boar was, indeed, said to be the very one which killed Adonis, the beautiful youth who was the favourite of Aphrodite. She, in a moment of anger, blinded Erymanthus, a mortal son of Apollo, because he saw her bathing, and in revenge Apollo sent the Boar, which gashed Adonis in the thigh, and killed him. When Adonis had died in her arms, Aphrodite wished to be revenged on the Boar, and had it brought before her tightly bound, though indeed it came willingly.

'Vilest of all wild beasts!' cried Aphrodite, 'was it indeed you who gashed the thigh of my beautiful Adonis?'

'I did it,' answered the Boar, 'but not out of any hatred. For when I saw Adonis, I loved him and ran to kiss him, even as I had seen you do. In my devotion I forgot about my sharp tusks, and one of these it was that wounded him.'

Hearing this, Aphrodite forgave the Boar, and set it free

to wander on Erymanthia, where in time it became so fierce and savage that no one dared go near it, or live on the slopes of the mountain.

Yet Heracles set out undaunted, and on the way met with a Centaur called Pholus. These Centaurs were men only to the waist, below that they had the body and legs of a horse. Some of them were very wise, for, though not immortal, they lived to a great age; but the wisest of all was Chiron.

Pholus entertained Heracles hospitably in his cave, setting roast meat before him. But he foolishly opened a jar of wine which Dionysus had left in the cave, and the wild Centaurs who lived near by, attracted by the smell, came crowding round, drank the strong wine, and were so maddened by it that they attacked Heracles. He was forced to shoot several of them with his poisoned arrows, and to drive the rest away. One of them, called Nessus, never forgave Heracles, but swore vengeance upon him, which he carried out in a strange fashion many years later.

After the battle Pholus picked up one of the arrows, marvelling that so little a thing could kill so great a creature as a Centaur. As he examined it, the arrow slipped from his fingers and pricked him in the foot; and the poison of the Hydra on its tip was so strong that he died in a few minutes.

Heracles grieved sorely when he saw that the kindly

Centaur was dead, and buried him with all honour before continuing on his way in search of the Boar, which he caught by chasing it into a deep snow-drift, plunging in after it, and tying its legs firmly together.

When he arrived at Tiryns with the Boar and flung it down for inspection, Eurystheus was so terrified that he jumped into a large brass pot and hid at the bottom of it, gibbering with fear, until Heracles took the creature away. He flung it into the sea and it swam away to Italy, and its tusks were preserved ever after in the temple of Apollo at Cumae.

As soon as the coast was clear, Eurystheus emerged from his jar, and sent Heracles off on his next Labour:

'I won't have any more dangerous animals brought back this time!' he declared. 'But I've thought of a thoroughly nasty job for you, and one that's absolutely impossible. Go to King Augeas over at Elis – he has the biggest herd of cattle of any man in Greece, thousands of them. Clean out his stables in a single day; they are rather dirty, as they've not been touched for thirty years!'

Off went Heracles, determined to accomplish this Labour too, however unpleasant and difficult it might be, and after careful examination he hit upon a scheme.

But first of all he went to King Augeas and, without saying anything about Eurystheus, declared:

'I'll undertake to clear your cattle-stables, yard and all, in a single day, while your cows are out on the pasture, if you'll promise to give me a tenth of your herd in payment.'

Believing that what he offered was quite impossible, Augeas agreed to the bargain and swore solemnly to fulfil his side of it if the task was performed.

Heracles at once knocked holes in either end of the great stable-building, and by digging a short channel turned the courses of the rivers Alpheus and Peneus which flowed close by, so that both streams ran in through one gap and out through the other.

The strong current of water cleared out the thirty years' accumulation of dung in a very short time, and Heracles had turned back the rivers into their normal beds and rebuilt the gaps in the stable walls before the herds were driven home in the evening.

Augeas, however, refused to fulfil his side of the bargain, and Heracles had to return some years later to punish him. He did not reap any reward from Eurystheus either, who said that this Labour did not count, since Heracles had worked for hire, and packed him off to chase away the Stymphalian Birds.

These were the property of Ares: they had brazen claws, wings, and beaks, could moult their feathers at will – which sped down like sharp arrows – and ate human flesh. Athena advised Heracles not to go near them, for, so sharp were their beaks that by flying straight at a man they could pierce even the hardest armour. But she lent him a pair of brazen castanets, which Hephaestus had made specially, and he went up on to a mountain overlooking the deep pool of Stymphalus which was surrounded by dense woods.

When Heracles clashed the castanets the noise, helped by the echo, was so terrible that the Birds flew up in fear, and fled shrieking and clapping their wings to the distant island of Aretias, where Heracles was to meet them again when he went voyaging with the Argonauts.

As they fled he was able to bring down several of the Stymphalian Birds with his deadly arrows, and these he brought back in triumph to Eurystheus.

'That was a poor exploit!' he scoffed, kicking the dead birds contemptuously. 'No one could be afraid of harmless little creatures like this: I wish I'd known before I sent you after them. However, off you go now, and bring me the Cretan Bull.'

Heracles turned without a word, strode down to the harbour at Nauplia, and took ship to the beautiful island of Crete, where King Minos welcomed him warmly and entertained him in his great palace at Cnossus with its many stairs and passages, its strange, short columns with broad tops and narrow bases painted vivid reds and blues, and the running water and sanitation which were not to be surpassed until three thousand years later.

Minos gladly gave Heracles permission to take the Bull. 'It is causing havoc all over the island,' he told him. 'The fault is mine, I'm afraid. Poseidon sent it to me out of the sea so that I might offer up a worthy sacrifice, but, in my greed and folly, I kept it myself and substituted one of my own bulls. After that it went mad, and now no one can do anything with it.'

Heracles, however, was a match for any mad bull. He captured this one without any difficulty and carried it away to Greece. When he reached Tiryns he let the Bull loose, and Eurystheus only just got into his jar in time, and crouched there gibbering with fear for several days.

But the Bull, failing to get hold of Eurystheus, fled away north, crossed the Isthmus of Corinth, and came to Marathon, beyond Athens. Here it found the pastures green and tasty, and decided to stay there, killing anyone who came near it.

Unfortunately one of its first victims was a son of Minos, who happened to be visiting Athens, and Minos would not believe that he had been killed by the Bull. So he invaded Athens, and only made peace when King Aegeus agreed to send an offering of seven youths and seven maidens every year to be devoured by the Minotaur, a monster, half bull and half man, which lived in the Labyrinth, a maze which the clever craftsman Daedalus had made.

For twenty-seven years the Cretan Bull plagued the people of Marathon, and the Athenians regularly sent the tribute of youths and maidens to Minos, until Theseus came to Athens. But meanwhile Heracles was waiting in Tiryns for Eurystheus to recover from his fright; and when at last he did, the new Labour which he had devised for him was to journey north in Thrace and bring back the horses of King Diomedes.

'Only be sure you tame them before they reach Argolis,' insisted Eurystheus, 'for they are terrible creatures, which are fed only on the flesh of men!'

So Heracles set out; but on his way a strange adventure befell him, when he stopped to visit the young Prince Admetus of Pherae in Thessaly.

CHAPTER ELEVEN

The Story of Admetus

Oh, a House that loves the stranger,
  And a House for ever free!
And Apollo, the Song-changer,
  Was a herdsman in thy fee;
    Yea, a-piping he was found
    Where the upland valleys wound,
To the kine from out the manger
  And the sheep from off the lea,
    And love was upon Othrys at the sound.

EURIPIDES
Alcestis (Translated by Gilbert Murray)

11

In the days when Heracles was still living happily at Thebes, there was a beautiful Princess called Alcestis who was the daughter of Pelias, King of Iolcus. She was so beautiful that many princes came to ask her hand in marriage and Pelias, who did not wish to anger the rest by choosing one of them, said that he would only give her to the man who could yoke a wild boar and a lion to his chariot and drive safely round the race-course.

Of all the young princes, Admetus of Pherae was the bravest and most handsome, and Alcestis loved him alone. But her father would not let them marry unless

Admetus fulfilled the condition which he had made.

Now just before he came to woo Alcestis, a strange herdsman had come to him and begged to serve him for one year without wages. Admetus readily agreed to this, and being a good and amiable prince he treated his servant kindly and well. The herdsman served faithfully, and the herds of Admetus grew and prospered in the most remarkable way: for not one of his livestock died or was killed by wild beasts during that year, and all the cows had twin calves, and gave cream instead of milk.

One day, when the year was nearing its end, Admetus went up on to Mount Othrys to seek his herdsman, and saw a strange sight. In a green valley shaded by pine trees the herdsman sat playing on his pipes more sweetly than any mortal minstrel; and as he played the streaky-golden lynxes and the tawny-coated lions, drawn by his music, came and rubbed their heads against him, while the shy fawns danced and frisked in and out of the shadows, fearing neither the lions nor the man who piped to them so magically.

Admetus stood at the edge of the glade overcome with awe and wonder, and seeing him the herdsman smiled, and said:

'Prince Admetus, do not be afraid nor surprised at what you see, for now that my servitude is almost ended I can tell you that I am none other than Apollo, the Immortal son of Zeus. Listen, and I will tell you how it comes about that I, an Immortal, am servant to a mortal man.

'My son Asclepius, whose mother was the mortal woman Coronis, by my will and with the aid of wise Chiron the Centaur, became the greatest healer and the most expert in the knowledge of medicine that the world has known. So skilled did he become that at length he discovered how to bring the dead to life – if only he could use his arts at the very moment of death. But Hades, Lord of the Dead, found that on account of my son's skill few new subjects were being added to his kingdom, and he accused Zeus of cheating him of his share in the bargain which was made between them at the beginning of the world.

'Then Zeus bade his servants the Cyclopes forge a thunderbolt, and when it was made he hurled it at Asclepius and struck him dead. In a moment of rage I seized my bow and arrows and slew those of the Cyclopes who had made the thunderbolt. Filled with righteous fury, Zeus would have cast me down into Tartarus; but my mother, the divine Leto, begged for my pardon, and Zeus decreed that I must become the slave of a mortal master for one year.

'So I came to you, Admetus; and I have not regretted my choice. For you have proved a fair and kindly master, and I will reward you in any way I can.'

When Admetus heard this, he remembered the condition on which Alcestis was to be won, and begged Apollo to help him, for he knew what a power he had over the wild beasts.

'I will certainly assist you in this,' Apollo assured him. 'But you must journey to Thebes and seek a young man called Heracles who will help in the taming of the lion and the boar.'

Admetus did as he was told; and with such assistance it was not long before he was driving in triumph to Iolcus behind his strange steeds, and bringing Alcestis back to Pherae as his bride.

The wedding was celebrated immediately, but in his excitement Admetus forgot to offer the usual sacrifice to Artemis. To punish him, she hid away Alcestis and in her place left a hissing coil of snakes.

But Apollo made haste to appease his sister, and not only restored Alcestis to her anxious husband, but as a reward to Admetus arranged that when Death came for him he need not obey that fearful summons if any other would consent to die in his place.

This was highly irregular, but Apollo managed it by making the Three Fates drunk with sweet wine. These were the three weird sisters whose task was to spin the thread of a man's life and cut it off at the proper time.

The time came sooner than was expected: Hades sent his messenger, Death, to the palace at Pherae, and Admetus turned anxiously to the only people likely to help him, his aged father and mother.

'You are old,' he said, 'you have lived long and enjoyed all that life has to offer. There is nothing for you to look forward to now except the pain, illness, and slow death to which old age comes.'

But neither of them was willing to face death in his place, and indeed his father answered angrily: 'I have no call to die! You say I have not many days to live, whatever happens: all the more reason for taking special care of myself and enjoying them as fully as possible! As for you, I call you a mere coward, seeking for someone else to die instead of you!'

But Death was waiting; and when Alcestis heard how Admetus could be saved, she gave herself up in his place, so great was her love, and nothing he could say would change her determination.

So, while Admetus and the whole household mourned and wept, Alcestis said goodbye to her husband and her children, and feeling herself grow weaker and weaker, lay down on her bed and died.

It was just at this moment that Heracles, on his way north in search of the horses of King Diomedes, arrived at the palace, and being an old friend of Admetus, knocked at the door and asked for hospitality.

Admetus honoured Heracles more highly than any of his friends, and moreover among the Greeks hospitality was one of the most sacred duties of a good man.

So he welcomed Heracles into the palace, saw to it that he had a good meal with plenty of wine, and told him nothing about what was happening.

'But surely you're in mourning?' objected Heracles. 'Is it your old father? Or your mother who has died?'

'They both live yet,' answered Admetus.

'Is it then some relation?' asked Heracles, who did not even think that it might be Alcestis.

'It's a foreign woman, not related to me in blood,' said Admetus carefully.

'Well, if that is all,' replied Heracles, much relieved, 'I'll accept your hospitality, though I know it's burdensome when guests come to a house of mourning.'

'Whoever had died,' said Admetus firmly, 'you should still find a ready welcome here. The guest chamber is far away from the place of mourning, so we will not distress you with any sounds of grief.'

Only half satisfied, Heracles, who was weary after his long journey, settled down to supper, ate well, and drank a large quantity of wine.

Meanwhile Admetus and the mourners left the palace, carrying the body of Alcestis on a bier towards the burial ground at some distance from the city.

They were hardly out of sight when Heracles came striding out of the guest-room, a wreath round his head, singing lustily. There he met the house steward, an old man who was devoted to Alcestis, and could not restrain his tears.

'How now!' cried Heracles jovially. 'What's all this about? Some foreign woman dead, and all the household glum and sullen! That's not the way to welcome a guest, particularly not your master's old friend and comrade in arms. Your master and mistress are both alive and well, so all this mourning seems rather excessive!'

'Alive!' sobbed the old steward. 'Man, have you not heard?'

'Why yes, your master told me. A foreign woman, he said.'

'Oh, foreign by birth, certainly . . .'

'What is it? Some real grief which your master has hidden from me?' Heracles was beginning to grow suspicious. 'Speak, I command you!'

'Yes,' answered the steward, awed by the fierceness of his tone. 'A real grief indeed: the Princess Alcestis has died.'

'Alcestis? And he welcomed me in and feasted me?' Heracles was overcome.

'He held it shame to turn you away,' answered the steward.

'So.' Heracles stood in deep thought. 'For my friend, who has treated me so nobly,' he said at last, 'I will dare anything . . . Where lies the tomb? Where shall I find Alcestis now?'

He spoke in a roar of anger, and the steward told, trembling, then fled back into the house while Heracles, flinging his lion-skin about him, strode away over the steep hillside.

Admetus had already returned to the palace by a longer way round when Heracles reached the graveyard, so that he had the place to himself.

But he was not quite alone, for there, standing by the tomb was a dark-robed figure which, being half an Immortal, Heracles was able to see. The tomb was open, and the figure was bending over the body of Alcestis with a drawn sword in his hand, about to cut off a lock of her hair.

'Stay, Death!' cried Heracles in his great voice. 'What do you there?'

The tall, solemn figure rose slowly and turned his dark, baleful eyes upon Heracles.

'I come for mine own,' he answered in a cold, hissing voice. 'Once this grey sword of mine has touched the hair of any mortal, that soul belongs to Hades, my Lord and Master.'

'Will you not this once release your victim?' asked Heracles. 'You know how and why she has come into your power: surely the Lady of your Lord, the Divine Maiden, Persephone, would willingly send back to earth the soul of a wife who has died, so young and so lovely, to save her husband?'

There was some truth in this, and the dark servant of Hades paused in thought. Then, with a grim smile, he laid down his sword:

'Heracles,' he said, 'I know you well, you whose mighty deeds are spoken of even in the dark Land of the Dead.

So come now, I will wrestle with you for the soul of Alcestis: many men have fought against Death, but none has ever conquered him!'

Then Heracles flung off his lion-skin and advanced unarmed to grapple with his dark adversary. Then there was such a wrestling match as had never been known before, or is likely to be seen again. To and fro they reeled and struggled, the cold arms of Death locked round Heracles and his icy breath coming in great gasps.

But Heracles had him round the waist, and his mighty arms closed tighter and tighter until he felt Death's ribs cracking in his grip. At last Death admitted himself beaten and departed to his own place, moaning direfully. But Alcestis sat up in the tomb, and when Heracles took her by the hand she stepped out and followed him, walking like one in a dream.

Casting the veil over her face, Heracles led her back to the palace, and found Admetus plunged in grief, blaming himself most bitterly that he had ever let Alcestis die for him.

'I have returned,' said Heracles, 'to ask a favour of you. I am going on a wild and hazardous adventure: will you guard this woman for me until my return? Let her be a handmaiden in your house.'

But Admetus would not have her: she reminded him too much of Alcestis. So Heracles soon gave up his little trick and told his friend the whole truth.

'She will not speak for three days,' he warned Admetus. 'She has dwelt with Death, and cannot come back to this world all in a moment. But do not fear: she is no ghost but Alcestis herself, and in a little while will be as if she had never taken your place when Death came for you.'

Full of gratitude, Admetus begged his friend to stay and feast with them, but Heracles shook his head:

'I have feasted,' he said. 'Now I must be on my way: there is but little rest for me in this world.'

He turned resolutely and went north, ever north, until he came to the wild land of Thrace. There Diomedes welcomed him kindly: but Heracles knew that it was only a pretence, since it was this savage king's custom to throw his guests to the four terrible horses, who would immediately devour them.

Next day, with the help of a groom belonging to Diomedes, Heracles managed to steal the four horses, and even to harness them to a chariot, though they had never before known bit or bridle.

But the groom then betrayed him to Diomedes, who followed him with a band of men. Heracles, when he saw them coming, left the groom to hold the horses, and broke down a stretch of the sea wall. It was high tide, and the great waves came pouring through, and washed away most of the Thracians.

King Diomedes, however, he captured and carried back to the chariot. There, finding that the horses had already eaten the treacherous groom, he threw the wicked king to them as well, and they devoured him also.

After this Heracles drove off at full speed, and whether it was through eating their master, or whether he managed to tame them on the way, certain it is that when they reached Tiryns, Eurystheus had no need to hide himself in his brass jar.

The horses were quite tame now, and Eurystheus dedicated them to Hera. But they continued to be the strongest and most fearless horses in all Greece; and several of their descendants were used in the war against Troy.

As for Heracles, he was given no rest from labour: for Eurystheus sent him off again immediately – this time to bring back the belt of Hippolyta, the Queen of the Amazons, which his daughter greatly desired to possess. This belt was the gift of Ares, the Lord of War, to the bravest of the Amazons, who were a race of warrior women, trained to the use of arms and skilled particularly in casting the javelin and shooting with the bow.

They allowed no men in their wild land on the south coast of the Black Sea; and they kept their husbands in the next country, visiting them only for one month in every year.

To reach this land Heracles had to go by sea. So he gathered together a band of adventurers, and set sail for Troy and the Hellespont.

CHAPTER TWELVE

The Wanderings of Heracles

. . . Now he goes
With no less presence, but with much more love,
Than young Alcides when he did redeem
The virgin tribute paid by howling Troy
To the sea monster . . . Go, Hercules!
Live thou, I live: – with much, much more dismay
I view the fight than thou that makest the fray!

SHAKESPEARE
The Merchant of Venice

12

Heracles sailed from Nauplia in Argolis with nine companions, amongst whom were two young heroes named Peleus and Telamon, who were both to win great fame in days to come.

After several adventures on the way, they came into the Black Sea and arrived in the land of the Amazons. They prepared for war, but to their surprise Queen Hippolyta came down to the harbour to visit them in a friendly manner, and even offered to give Heracles the belt as soon as he explained why he had come.

But Hera, who had an eye on what Heracles was doing,

felt that this was far too easy a victory for him. So she disguised herself as an Amazon warrior and went hastening to the fortified citadel:

'Amazons, come swiftly!' she cried. 'There is a ship in the harbour filled with men, vile pirates, who have captured our queen and will carry her off to sell as a slave in Greece or Troy!'

The Amazons needed no second summons. Out they came like bees when their hive is disturbed, and with fierce cries rushed down to the shore and attacked Heracles and his companions.

Terrible was the battle that followed: great were the deeds done that day by Peleus and Telamon; but it was Heracles with his unerring arrows who slew the leaders of the Amazons, and at length captured Melanippe the Queen's favourite sister. When he threatened to kill her unless they gave him the girdle and let him sail away in safety, they obeyed Hippolyta and marched back to their city in great sorrow, while Heracles set sail for Greece in triumph.

On the return journey, as they sailed down the coast of Troy, a strange adventure befell them. As they passed near a pleasant inlet of the sea the sound of weeping came to their ears. Following the voice, and rowing gently, they found a lovely girl chained to a rock by the side of the water – just as Perseus had found Andromeda many years before.

Halting the ship close by, Heracles spoke to her:

'Maiden,' said he, 'who are you, and why are you chained here?'

'Alas,' she sobbed, 'I hang here, waiting a terrible fate, through no fault of my own. I am called Hesione, and my father is Laomedon the King of Troy. It is said that the great Immortals Poseidon and Apollo came to him, by the will of Zeus, as workmen, and with their own hands built the walls of Troy city, which is called Ilion after Ilus his father, the son of Tros, Dardanus's grandson. King Laomedon swore to pay them well; but when the work was done, he broke his oath, refusing to pay anything and threatening to sell his two workmen as slaves, after cutting off their ears, if they did not immediately depart from Troy. Then the two Immortals revealed themselves, and in their anger Apollo sent a pestilence which has devastated the country, and Poseidon sent a sea-serpent which comes at high tide to prey upon the people. So Laomedon has bound me here as an offering, for he hopes that my life will buy Poseidon's forgiveness.

'Noble sir, you seem a mighty man, skilled in arms: I beg you to save me from the serpent. For very soon he will come!'

Then Heracles beached his ship, and on the shore King Laomedon met him.

'What will you give me,' asked Heracles, 'If I kill this monster and save your daughter and your land?'

'If you save my daughter, you may have her as your

wife,' answered Laomedon, 'and if you kill the monster, I will give you the magic horses which Zeus gave to my grandfather when he took Ganymede to Olympus.'

Now Ganymede was a handsome young prince of Troy whom Zeus had chosen to be cup-bearer to the Immortals and assist his daughter Hebe in waiting on them as they feasted in golden Olympus. So he sent a great eagle to carry Ganymede up to heaven; and he gave Tros in exchange two magic white horses which could run over the sea or the standing corn as lightly and as swiftly as the wind.

Heracles agreed to this, and when the Trojans had built him a low wall by the sea-shore, he crouched down behind it to lie in wait for the monster.

Scarcely was he ready, when far out to sea he saw a line of white foam, and heard a strange roaring which drew nearer and nearer. Then he saw the monster itself, its eyes flashing and flickering beneath the blue-grey film of its eyelids, and its three rows of mighty teeth gleaming in its huge mouth. It came with head and neck raised high above the water and the long coils of its scaly body curling and rippling in great arches.

Heracles lay behind his wall until the great Sea Serpent reared up its head over the shore, roaring and hissing with rage. Then Hesione shrieked with terror and, as the Serpent turned to seize her, Heracles leapt up on the wall, uttering a fierce war cry, and began loosing swift arrows at the creature's head and neck.

The Serpent minded them no more than a mountain minds the raindrops which beat on its rocky sides; but when Heracles, seeing how useless the arrows were, dropped his bow and began pelting the monster with great rocks and boulders, it turned away from the screaming maiden and came towards him, roaring with rage, its great mouth wide open.

Then Heracles cried to Zeus for help and, drawing his sword, leapt straight into the Serpent's mouth, just avoiding the three rows of razor-sharp teeth, and charged down its throat, hacking and hewing with his sword.

The Serpent screamed horribly and, while all the watching Trojans cried aloud with terror and pity, it closed its jaws and plunged down under the waves. But they saw that its great coils were twisting and writhing beneath the water, and before long it lay dead on the sand. Then the water was suddenly red with blood, and it bubbled above the corpse, and Heracles rose to the surface, gasping for breath, having cut his way out through the Serpent's side.

Telamon and Peleus cheered loudly, and guided the ship quickly towards him. He clambered on board, and they rowed to the rock where Hesione was still tied, and cut her bonds.

Then they brought her to the shore, and King Laomedon met them, already planning treachery in his evil heart.

'Come to my city,' he said, 'so that we may feast after

this mighty exploit. Then you may rest safely, and sail away tomorrow carrying my daughter and the magic horses.' But he intended to murder them all that night as they slept.

Heracles, though he suspected nothing, replied:

'I cannot stay now, King Laomedon, for my Labours must be accomplished. But I will return to claim my reward, never fear. So keep the horses safely for me, and keep my bride-to-be also.'

Then he set sail, and after several more adventures arrived safely at Tiryns where Eurystheus received the Belt of the Amazon Queen for his daughter, and sent Heracles straight out again – this time to fetch back, without either asking or paying for them, the cattle of Geryon, who was said to be the strongest man in the world. This ogre had been born with three heads and six arms and hands, but only one body from the waist downwards. He lived on the mysterious island of Erythia in the Atlantic Ocean beyond the Straits of Gibraltar.

Heracles set out on this expedition alone, and journeyed overland through Italy, France, and Spain, slaying many wild beasts and other monsters on the way, until he came to the straits separating Europe from Africa.

Here he set up two great stone pillars, one at Gibraltar and the other at Ceuta: and the Straits were called the Pillars of Hercules by the Romans in consequence.

As he laboured to raise the pillar on the African coast, the heat was terrific and Heracles, half crazed by the sun's tropical glare, set an arrow to his bow and loosed it with all his strength in the direction of the Sun-chariot which the Titan Helios was at that moment bringing down towards the western ocean.

Helios was so tickled by the audacity of this struggling mortal that he not only veiled his beams immediately, but lent Heracles his magic goblet of pure gold, shaped like a gigantic water-lily.

In this Heracles crossed to the island of Erythia, using his lion-skin as a sail. On reaching the shore his first care was to moor his strange boat in a concealed inlet: then he climbed a hill in the centre of the island to spy out the land. He had scarcely reached the summit, when a great dog came rushing at him open-mouthed, only to meet his end from a single blow of the deadly club.

As he descended in the direction of the pastures where he could see the beautiful red cattle grazing, Heracles was attacked by the herdsman, whom he killed also, but only after a fierce fight. Heracles then drove the cattle towards the shore, but before he reached it the ogre Geryon came rushing towards him, brandishing various weapons in his six huge hands, and shouting threats of terrible vengeance.

Heracles knew that he was no match for so powerful a monster if they came to hand-grips; so, quick as thought, he discharged three arrows one after another, one through each of the ogre's three throats: and that was the end of him. Then he drove the cattle into the magic goblet, sailed back to Spain, and having returned his strange vessel to Helios with many thanks, began the weary task of driving the herd overland all the way back to Greece.

On the way many adventures befell him. Once in the south of France near where Marseille now stands, he was attacked by a large army of warlike natives. He fought and fought until all his arrows were spent, and then it seemed that his end had come, for the ground was soft with not a stone in sight. In despair, Heracles prayed to Zeus, who took pity on him and rained down stones from above, thus supplying him with ample ammunition. That great plain covered with smooth round stones may be seen to this very day.

On another occasion Heracles camped for the night in a valley among seven low hills where now stands the city of Rome. He did not know that a fire-breathing troll called Cacus lived in a huge cave under mount Aventine, nor did he realize in the morning that this creature had come down during the night and stolen several of the cattle. For Cacus had carefully blotted out all the foot-marks, and the mouth of his cave was hidden by a great door of solid rock which slid down in grooves.

But just as Heracles was setting out in the morning, he heard a cow lowing somewhere in the hillside: for Cacus had very foolishly taken one of the cows who had a calf, and left the calf with the herd.

Heracles at once counted the cattle, found that some were

missing, and set out to deal with the thief. Before long he found the door of the cavern, but Cacus, realizing that he was discovered, hastily broke the chains and balances which should have raised it, and even Heracles could not lift the enormous block of stone and slide it up its grooves.

Three times Heracles strove to stir it, and three times drew back, gnashing his teeth with rage. But after the third attempt, as Cacus laughed triumphantly within, Heracles saw that there was a crack in the hillside above the cave. He climbed up to it, set his heels in it and his back against the hill itself, and pushed with all his might. The crack slowly widened, and then with a sudden roar the whole side of the hill slid away and a great mass of rock went crashing down into the river at the foot.

But Heracles landed on the floor of the cavern, which was now open to the light of day for the first time, and rushed to attack Cacus. The troll immediately filled the hollow with smoke which he belched out of his mouth; but Heracles plunged valiantly into the thick of it, guided by the flames which Cacus was breathing, and caught him by the throat. Very soon the fight was over, and Heracles, singed and choking from the smoke, dragged the troll's body out into the open. Then he gathered the missing cattle and continued on his way.

One more strange adventure befell him as he drew near to the north of Greece, for Hera sent a giant gadfly which stung the cattle and scattered them far and wide. Heracles pursued them relentlessly, and at length, having retrieved nearly all of them, he lay down to rest in a cave somewhere in the hills of the country now called Bulgaria, on the west coast of the Black Sea.

It was cold and stormy, and Heracles slept long and heavily after his laborious search for the cattle. But in the morning he found that the horses which drew his chariot had mysteriously disappeared.

In a great fury he wandered far and wide until at length he came to another cave, in which he found a mysterious creature. She was like a woman from the waist upward, but below that was a scaly snake. He looked at her in wonder, but asked nevertheless:

'Strange maiden, have you seen my horses?'

'Yes,' she replied, 'it was I who took them in when they strayed this way. But I will never give them up to you, unless you wed me, according to the custom of this country. Here we are married when we have kissed thrice; and the marriage lasts only for as long as we both wish it.'

There was no help for it, so Heracles kissed the snake-maiden three times, and lodged in her cave for three days.

At the end of that time she gave him back his horses, and before leaving he strung the spare bow which he carried with him and gave it to her, saying:

'Lady, I prophesy that you will have three sons: let the one who can draw this bow as I do, come and seek me if he wishes for assistance in winning his fortune. But if he does not come, then let him, and no other, rule over this land after you.'

Then Heracles set out once more, and this time he reached Greece safely with the cattle.

But as he was crossing the isthmus of Corinth, a giant bandit who had taken possession of the place and stopped all travellers to rob or kill them, held him up:

'Hand all those cattle over to me!' he cried, 'and you shall pass in safety.'

'Never,' replied Heracles briefly.

Then the bandit picked up a huge rock and hurled it at him. Heracles dodged the great whirling mass, and picking it up flung it back with such good aim that the bandit never again molested travellers.

So Heracles came to Tiryns and handed over the cattle to Eurystheus.

'Now!' he cried, 'I have accomplished the Ten Labours which you set me, and spent more than eight years of my life in doing so: now I may go free!'

'Not so,' answered Eurystheus, 'for you know that two Labours do not count. Iolaus helped you to kill the Lernean Hydra, and you cleaned the Augean Stables for hire. So Hera commands that you perform two further Labours. Go now and bring back three Golden Apples from the Garden of the Hesperides!'

Once again Heracles bowed to his fate and with a weary sigh turned his back on Tiryns and set off once more.

CHAPTER THIRTEEN

The Golden Apples, and The Hound of Hell

Round and round the apples of gold,
  Round and round dance we;
Thus do we dance from the days of old
  About the enchanted tree;
Round, and round, and round we go,
While the spring is green, or the stream shall
  flow,
  Or the wind shall stir the sea!

After PINDAR
Tenth Pythian Ode (Translated by Andrew Lang)

13

Heracles set out wearily on his eleventh Labour without any idea of where the Golden Apples were to be found. But Zeus was watching him, since he had a special deed for him to perform which, as it turned out, did more to save both mortals and Immortals than any help which Heracles could give in the coming war with the Giants.

For all this while, Prometheus the good Titan had been lying chained to Mount Caucasus in punishment for disobeying Zeus by bringing fire to mankind. And the great eagle still came every day to devour his liver, which still grew again every night: but in spite of all his suffering, Prometheus still refused to tell Zeus of the danger greater than that of the Giants, which was threatening him.

Nevertheless, Zeus had grown merciful with time. If Prometheus had suffered in body, Zeus had suffered in mind – for he knew that at any moment he might make the mistake of which Prometheus had prophesied, and which only Prometheus could prevent.

So when Heracles came into the land of Illyria and begged the nymphs who lived there to tell him how he might find the Golden Apples, they replied that, by the command of their father, Zeus, he must journey on, to Mount Caucasus, and ask Prometheus.

The way was long and dangerous, but at length Heracles came to the great mountain above the world's end. Climbing by chasm and crevasse, by steep glissade and slippery glacier, he came to the great cliff-face on which the Titan was chained. And as he clambered up beside him, the great eagle swooped down to its horrible feast, and the mighty Titan screamed aloud in his agony.

But Heracles, with a shout of rage and pity, fitted an arrow to his bow, drew it to the head, and loosed it with all his might. The great eagle flew up, transfixed by the arrow, and plunged down into the black waves thousands of feet below.

'Who are you, rash mortal?' asked Prometheus slowly.

'I am Heracles, the son of Zeus,' was the answer. 'And

I come here by his command, to free you. For Zeus forgives you for your great crimes against himself, and asks your pardon for the torture to which he has put you. Nevertheless, he bids me say that, since his great decrees cannot be broken altogether, you must wear a ring on your finger for ever as a token that you are still bound in fetters of metal.'

Prometheus nodded his head and smiled:

'You are the Hero of whom I prophesied,' he said. 'Your hand shall strike down the Giants and save Olympus from ruin. But that you would come to set me free, I did not know, for a prophet cannot foretell his own future. But come, strike off my fetters and let me girdle my finger with the ring; and in memory of my sufferings I declare that mankind shall ever after wear rings in token of this day.'

Heracles set to work; and while he hacked and twisted at the brazen fetters he told Prometheus of his quest and asked him about the Golden Apples of the Hesperides.

'They grow on the tree which Mother Earth gave to Hera as a wedding present,' said Prometheus, 'and that tree is in a magic garden on the world's western verge, beyond the mountain on which my brother Atlas stands for ever supporting the starry sky on his shoulders. The dragon Ladon curls round that tree, and in the garden dwell the immortal daughters of Hesperus, the warden of the Evening Star, which is also the Star of the Morning; and he is the son of Atlas. Ask Atlas to assist you: for no mortal may enter that garden without great danger; and he has built a great wall round it that cannot be climbed.'

Many other things Prometheus told to Heracles, so that when his work was ended he went on his way with bowed head, thinking of the greatness and nobility of the mighty Titan, helper of mankind.

Once again Heracles met with many adventures as he traversed the earth on his quest: but there is not time now to tell how he fought with Cycnus the son of Ares, slew him and wounded even the Immortal Warlord himself; nor how in Egypt the cruel King Busiris who sacrificed all strangers came to find himself bound and offered up on his own altar; nor even of his adventures with the King of Ethiopia. But as he traversed Libya on his way to Mount Atlas, his strength was put to the proof in the hardest wrestling match of his whole career. For there dwelt the savage Antaeus, a giant son of Earth, who challenged all strangers to wrestle with him; and when he had killed them with his mighty hands, he used their skulls to decorate the temple of Poseidon. He lived in a cave and slept on the bare earth; and he would rob the lionesses of their cubs and eat them raw for his supper.

Heracles needed no second bidding when Antaeus challenged him to wrestle. He flung off his lion-skin, anointed himself all over with oil, and stood ready. Antaeus did the same, but in place of oil he covered himself from head to foot in dust.

Then they seized hold of one another, arms twisting with arms, bending and swaying backwards and forwards, striving to reach each other's throat with their clutching fingers. Heracles proved the stronger, and with a mighty effort flung the almost fainting Antaeus to the ground.

But then an amazing thing happened. The moment Antaeus touched the earth all his weariness passed from him, and he sprang to his feet with a shout of triumph, as fresh and strong as at the beginning of the battle.

Astonished, Heracles closed with him once more, and with a great effort flung him to the ground again. Up jumped the young giant with his strength and vigour again renewed, and Heracles exclaimed:

'A Son of Earth, are you? I might have guessed from whence you drew your strength! Come on again, and this time I'll see to it that we fight standing: if fall you must, fall upon me, and see what sort of vigour I can impart to you!'

Again they wrestled, and this time Heracles exerted his great strength and lifted Antaeus above his head, and held him there in spite of all his struggles, and did not lower him even when he grew weaker and weaker. But at last he took him in his arms, still careful that not so much as a toe touched the ground, and hugged him to death as a bear might.

Flinging aside the corpse of his cruel foe, Heracles continued on his way, and came soon to the great mountain, the highest in the known world, on top of which stood Atlas the Titan, holding up the sky lest it should sink down again upon the earth as it had done in the beginning of the world.

'I come to you for help, great Titan,' cried Heracles when he had climbed to the peak on which Atlas stood. 'Your brother Prometheus advised me to ask your assistance: I am Heracles, and I come for three of the Golden Apples to deliver to my task-master, Eurystheus of Tiryns, who loads me with labours by command of Immortal Hera.'

'Heracles, son of Zeus,' answered Atlas, 'I was warned long ago of your coming by wise Themis, sister of my Titan father. I will do what you wish if you will perform two great deeds to assist me. While I am away you must take my place and hold the sky upon your shoulders; and before you do this, you must slay the dragon Ladon who guards the tree; for even I may not touch the fruit while he lives.'

Heracles looked down beyond the mountain, towards the Western Ocean, and saw far below him the lovely Garden of the Hesperides. There were the cool glades and the silver leaves of Paradise, and in the midst the great Tree shining with the golden fruit, while three lovely nymphs, the daughters of Hesperus, danced and sang in the dappled sunlight.

Then he saw the Dragon curled about the tree, a monster longer than any he had slain, its scales shining with gold and blue. He drew an arrow from his quiver, fitted it to his bow, and shot with so unerring an aim that it pierced the Dragon's throat. The creature uncurled from the tree and glided away into the bushes, there to die slowly and strangely, for its tail was still alive several years later when the Argonauts visited the spot.

When Ladon the Dragon had gone, Atlas shifted his mighty burden on to the broad shoulders of Heracles, and stretching himself with a great sigh of relief, he hurried off in the direction of the Garden.

The hours passed slowly for Heracles as he stood there holding up his gigantic burden, and he felt weary and ill at ease as the light faded and the stars began twinkling in his hair. All through the long night he stood there, supporting the sky, and in the morning he could have shouted for joy when he saw Atlas striding up the mountain carrying three Golden Apples in his hand.

But his heart sank suddenly when the Titan stood still at a little distance and looked at him with a cruel gleam in his eyes.

'Here are the Apples,' said Atlas. 'But I will take them to King Eurystheus myself. I have been through great dangers to obtain them, it is only fair that I should have a sufficient respite from my burden. You cannot know what joy it is to walk the earth again, and feel no longer that heavy weight upon my shoulders.'

'You do indeed deserve your holiday,' answered Heracles, thinking quickly, 'and I wish you all joy of it, though I look forward to your return, for this is certainly a very heavy load. But when you set it upon my shoulders, I thought it was to remain there only a few hours, and I paid little attention to how it was placed. Now you, who have supported it so long, must be an expert sky-carrier: can you teach me how to arrange the burden most easily?'

'I can indeed,' replied the slow-witted Atlas, 'you should hold it like this – let me show you.'

He dropped the Golden Apples and, stepping forward eagerly, took the sky on his shoulders once more, explaining as he did so what was the easiest way to hold it up.

Heracles watched carefully: 'You know,' he said gravely, 'you do it so much better than I . . . I think I'd better leave you to it, and myself take those Golden Apples to Eurystheus. Every man to his own task!'

With that he set off down the mountain, leaving Atlas to lament the loss of his only chance of freedom.

When he reached the sea coast, Heracles took ship for Greece and after a long voyage was landed at Lindos on the island of Rhodes. He was so ravenously hungry after the journey that he killed the first ox he came upon, and roasted a great dinner for himself. But the owner of the ox stood on the lovely hillside where the castle of Lindos stands today, and cursed the stranger for an hour without stopping.

Heracles paid for the ox when he had eaten it. But in after days when the people of Lindos honoured Heracles as an Immortal, they always invoked him with curses instead of prayers in memory of his visit to their land.

Heracles went on his way to Tiryns when his hunger was satisfied, and delivered the Golden Apples to Eurystheus. That cowardly king was afraid to receive them, in case Hera should take vengeance on him, and said:

'I'll make you a present of them. You deserve them after so much trouble! You've only one more Labour to perform, and if you return safely from that, I expect you'll need the Golden Apples!' He sniggered cruelly, for the final Labour was to be the hardest and most dangerous of all – no less than to descend into the Realm of Hades and bring back Cerberus, the three-headed Hound of Hell.

When Heracles heard this, he turned away in despair, and left Tiryns, still carrying the Golden Apples.

But Zeus again was watching over him, and sent Athena and Hermes to his help. First of all Heracles gave the Apples to the Goddess, who handed them over to Aphrodite to take care of for the time being. But when, later, Athena returned them to the Garden of the Hesperides, she took pity on Atlas and showed him the Gorgon's Head – and he became the topmost peak of stony Mount Atlas with great thankfulness.

Meanwhile the two Immortals led Heracles to the great cave at Taenarum, not far from Sparta, and down into the gloomy depths of the earth until they came to the Underworld which was bounded by the black River Styx. Here

Athena waited, while Hermes went on with Heracles, for it was one of his offices to lead souls down to Hades.

At the River Styx the dark old ferryman, Charon, was waiting with his boat. He was only allowed to ferry dead souls across that stream, and they paid him one coin, called an 'obol', which was always placed ready in a dead person's mouth. He would have refused to take this living passenger, but Heracles scowled at him so fiercely that he did not dare: and he was punished afterwards by Hades for his cowardice.

On the other side Heracles found himself in the grey, twilit land of the dead, where ghosts flitted about, moaning and gibbering.

The first he met was the Gorgon Medusa, and when he saw that terrible shape, he fitted an arrow to his bow; but Hermes reminded him with a smile that she was only a harmless ghost, killed by Perseus.

Heracles saw many terrible sights in the Realm of Hades, for he crossed the Fiery River of Phlegethon and entered Tartarus, the prison where the Titans lay, and where the wicked are punished.

He saw, for example, Ixion on his flaming wheel, the wicked king who had broken faith with Zeus; and Tantalus who stood up to the neck in cool water and yet could not quench his burning thirst since the water went away as soon as he stooped to drink. Also he saw Sisyphus, thief and murderer, whose doom was to roll a stone to the top of a hill down which it always rolled just as he neared the summit; and the daughters of King Danaus who murdered their husbands and had to fill for ever a cask which had a hole in the bottom.

Only one of the souls in torment was Heracles allowed to free; and that was Ascalaphus, who had given Persephone six pomegranate seeds when Hades first carried her down to his kingdom. If she had not eaten these, she could have returned to earth for ever: but since she had eaten in the realm of the dead, she was forced to return there for six months every year. So Demeter in fury placed a heavy stone on top of Ascalaphus; but Heracles was allowed to roll it away, and Ascalaphus was turned into an owl instead.

At last Heracles came to where Hades and Persephone sat in state, and he told them why he was there and begged them to lend him their terrible hound.

'You may willingly take Cerberus,' answered Hades, 'if you can overcome him without the use of weapons.'

So Heracles returned to the bank of the Styx, and Cerberus rushed at him, since he was there to prevent the souls of the dead from leaving the Realm of Hades. Cerberus had three mighty heads with lion-like manes bristling with snakes; and in place of a tail a serpent writhed and hissed. Heracles wrapped his lion-skin about himself, seized hold of the brute and squeezed him hard. Cerberus struggled and tried to bite; but the lion-skin was too tough, and Heracles was too strong. Only the serpent-tail managed to hurt him; but even then Heracles would not let go.

At last Cerberus gave way, and Heracles carried him off in triumph, crossing the Dark River with the help of Hermes and Athena. They led him up the great cavern near Troezen through which Dionysus had brought his mother Semele, and at last they saw the light of day.

To Heracles this was welcome, but when Cerberus beheld the glorious light of the sun, he struggled, and howled dismally, and the white foam flying from his jaws spattered all the grass. From this foam grew the flower called Aconite which gives the deadly poison known as Wolf's-bane.

Holding his captive firmly, Heracles set out at once for Tiryns. When he arrived there, he strode straight into the citadel, shouting for Eurystheus. And when the King appeared, Heracles cried:

'My last Labour is achieved! Here is Cerberus!'

He dropped the dog on the ground as he spoke, and it rushed at Eurystheus, barking with all three mouths and hissing with every snake on its three manes.

Eurystheus turned with a scream of terror and leapt into his brass pot, where he was still shrieking with fear when Heracles left Tiryns for the last time, carrying Cerberus in his arms.

Straight back to the Dark River of Styx he went, and

placed the terrible Hound of Hell on the gloomy shore. Then he returned to earth rejoicing, his Twelve Labours ended, free at last.

As before, Heracles came up from the Realm of Hades by the great gorge of Dionysus near Troezen; and he was so weary after his Labours that he went to visit his friend Pittheus who was king there.

As he entered the palace he took off his lion-skin and flung it over a chair, where it lay in a most life-like fashion. Presently a crowd of children came into the room laughing and talking. But when they saw the lion-skin they turned and fled, shrieking that there was a lion in the palace.

All except one. Pittheus had a grandson aged about seven, whose name was Theseus. He did not run away: on the contrary, he snatched an axe from one of the guards and attacked the skin furiously, thinking it was a live lion.

Heracles laughed encouragingly: 'We'll have you following in my footsteps before long!' he cried.

'I could ask for no better fate,' answered young Theseus stoutly.

CHAPTER FOURTEEN

THE ADVENTURES OF THESEUS

Give me again your empty boon,
  Sweet Sleep – the gentle dream
How Theseus 'neath the fickle moon
  Upon the Ocean stream
Took me and led me by the hand
To be his Queen in Athens land.

He slew the half-bull Minotaur
  In labyrinthine ways.
But, threadless, had he come no more
  From out my father's maze:
Yet I who taught his hands this guile
Am left forlorn on Naxos Isle.

NONNOS
Dionysiaca XLVII (Translated by R. L. G.)

14

The boy whom Heracles met at Troezen was the son of <u>Aegeus, King of Athens</u>, who had married Aethra the daughter of King Pittheus. Aegeus never saw his son as a child, for even before the babe was born, he was forced to return to Athens to fight for his throne against his three brothers who ought really to have been governing with him.

But before he left Troezen he lifted a great rock and placed under it a sword and a pair of sandals:

'If our child is a boy,' he said to Aethra, 'do not tell him who his father is until he can lift this stone. When that time comes, send him to me in Athens for I shall need his help.'

So Theseus was born in Troezen, and grew strong and brave, learning both wisdom and skill at all manly pursuits from his grandfather and his mother. He learnt much from Heracles also during his visit, and determined that when he was old enough he too would spend his life fighting against monsters and savage robbers, of whom there were still plenty in Greece.

It was not until he was eighteen that Theseus was able to lift the stone. When he did, and was told by Aethra that his father was King Aegeus, he buckled on both sword and sandals eagerly and prepared to set out for Athens.

'Go there in a swift ship,' begged Aethra. 'The distance is short, and the dangers few, but overland there are robbers; and your cousins, the fifty sons of Pallas, your father's youngest brother, will try to kill you so as to secure the rule of Athens for themselves.'

Theseus would not listen to such advice. 'If there are robbers on the road,' he said, 'I must go out of my way to fight and slay them. For that is what Heracles would have done if he were still in Greece.'

For at this time Heracles, having killed his friend Iphitus in a moment of fury had, as a punishment, been sold as a slave to Omphale, a queen in Asia, where he was forced to wear women's clothes and work at the loom – which was a far worse fate for him and much harder to endure than performing the Twelve Labours for Eurystheus.

So Theseus set out on the road to Athens, determined to clear the way of all evildoers: and he had not far to go before he met the first. A few miles from Troezen, at Epidaurus, where the most beautiful of ancient Greek theatres stands today, lived Periphetes the Clubman. He was lame, but what he lacked in his legs he made up for in the strength of his arms. His only weapon was a mighty club shod with iron, which was death to all passers by – until Theseus wrested it from his hands and paid him out in his own cruel coin.

This was always the method adopted by Theseus, for when he reached the isthmus of Corinth he dealt with Sinis the Pinebender in a similar way. This ruffian accosted Theseus as he approached:

'Sir stranger!' he cried. 'Come and test your strength by helping me bend down this pine tree!'

But Theseus knew what to expect, and when the tree was bent down in a great curve it was he and not Sinis who let go suddenly and sent his partner flying through the air. Then he bent down two trees himself, tied Sinis between them, and allowed them to tear him in half; for he saw the sad remains of former travellers dangling from the tree-tops on either side.

As he went on, Theseus stopped to kill a wild sow which was ravaging the lands just beyond the isthmus, and then on a rocky cliff where the path was narrow, with a sheer drop into the sea, he met Sciron.

'All who pass this way must pay a toll!' cried this brute rudely. 'So down on your knees, like your betters before you, and wash my feet!'

Now Theseus had been warned about Sciron; so he knelt down warily as far from the cliff edge as he could.

Then Sciron shouted: 'My turtle is hungry today – go down and feed it!' And as he spoke he kicked Theseus, meaning to push him over the edge into the sea. But Theseus was ready for him, and caught Sciron by the foot and flung him over his shoulder shouting:

'Go and feed your turtle yourself!' And Sciron went head first down the cliff into the deep water – and never had that turtle eaten a viler man.

Continuing along the coast road, Theseus came to Eleusis where mighty Cercyon wrestled with all comers and crushed their bones in his bear-like hug. But this time he met with a man stronger than himself, and presently he lay on his back upon the ground with all his ribs broken.

Whistling merrily at his success so far, Theseus strode on his way towards Athens, and came in the evening to a dark tower standing by the high road.

'Good evening to you, stranger!' cried the master of this place who was called Procrustes. 'You must be weary after a day's travel in the heat of the sun: come in and rest for the night – I insist upon it! All travellers come to partake of my hospitality, and to try my wonderful bed . . . What, you've never heard of the Bed of Procrustes? Ah, you've much to learn! It is a magic bed, and it fits all comers, great or small, long or short!'

Some say that an old servant, the only man who had really fitted that bed, warned Theseus of what to expect: but certain it is that when bed-time came Theseus turned suddenly upon his host and cried:

'Come, let me fit you to the bed first!' and flinging him down upon it, in spite of his cries and entreaties, he cut off first his feet and then his head which protruded over the ends – for even so had Procrustes done to all his unfortunate guests, lopping them if they were too long, and beating them out if they were too short as if they had been lumps of lead: and no man ever lived after a night on that terrible bed.

And so, having cleared the road of all these miscreants, Theseus came to Athens and strode into the palace of his father King Aegeus. He did not say at first who he was, nor show the sword and the sandals and only the Witch-wife who now ruled the old king knew him. Aegeus had taken her because she promised to make him the father of many sons who would grow up to defend him against his fifty nephews, the children of Pallas: but, once his wife, she kept him in such fear that he did whatever she commanded.

Now she warned him against this young stranger who professed to have done such mighty deeds for the glory of Athens, so that at last he said:

'Young man, I will believe what you say only if you bring me the Cretan Bull which wastes my land at Marathon, and kills my subjects.'

This was the Bull which Heracles had brought from Crete, and which Eurystheus had allowed to escape into Attica some years before.

Off went Theseus, full of confidence, and in spite of its terrible strength and fury, took the Bull by the horns and dragged it back to Athens, where he sacrificed it to Athena on the acropolis.

This was more than the Witch-wife could endure, and she mixed a cup of deadly poison for the feast that night, having warned Aegeus that the stranger came to murder him.

Theseus was determined to show the king who he was that very evening, and as he prepared to feast on the best sirloin from the Cretan Bull, he drew the sword to carve it, and laid it on the table in full view while he paused to drink, taking up the poisoned cup.

Aegeus saw the sword and recognized it. With a cry he dashed the cup from his son's hand, so that the poison was spilt on the floor, where it bubbled and hissed, eating its way into the solid stone.

Then the Witch-wife fled swiftly from Athens, and

Aegeus welcomed Theseus, and declared him to be the heir to his throne.

This did not please the sons of Pallas, and they gathered together their followers, meaning to attack Athens and kill him. But Theseus armed the Athenians, marched out of the city, ambushed his enemies and defeated them utterly.

When he returned to Athens, he was surprised to find the city in mourning:

'What does this mean?' he cried. 'Have I not just returned from a victory?'

Then Aegeus told him, with tears in his eyes, that the envoys from Crete had just arrived to carry off the tribute of seven youths and seven maidens to be fed to the Minotaur, as agreed when King Minos came to take vengeance for the death of his son whom the Bull had killed at Marathon.

When Theseus heard this he exclaimed: 'I will go myself as one of the young men, and meet with this Minotaur!'

In vain Aegeus begged him not to be so foolhardy: 'If I slay the Minotaur,' said Theseus, 'it will surely save our country from further tribute – so go I will.'

'Then promise me,' said Aegeus sadly, 'that if you return victorious you will hoist white sails on your ship: but if you do not, the black sails which waft the Athenian youths and maidens to their doom will tell me that you have perished with them.'

Promising this, Theseus set out for Crete, and in due time arrived at Cnossus where mighty Minos ruled. Here the victims were kindly entertained, and took part in racing and boxing contests before the king and his court. As he stood panting at the winning post, the Princess Ariadne saw Theseus and straightway loved him.

In great misery at the thought of the fate which awaited him, Ariadne at length thought of a scheme. That night she visited Theseus: 'Ask to go first into the Labyrinth tomorrow,' she instructed him. 'No one has ever found his way out again, but if you can take with you this clue of thread, without it being discovered, and fasten one end to the door when it is closed after you, unrolling it as you go, you may find your way back by means of it. I will be at the door at midnight to let you out if you are successful: but you must take me with you in your flight, for I will not be safe here when it is known that I helped you.'

Theseus did exactly as he was told, and next day entered the Labyrinth with the clue of thread concealed in his hand. When alone, he attached one end to the lintel of the door, and unwound the thread behind him as he traced his way through the winding passages, leading up and down, hither and thither, until he came to the great chamber or cavern in the centre where the dim light from above showed the monster waiting for him.

The Minotaur was a fearsome creature with a great human body and the head and neck of a bull. Its skin was as tough as the toughest leather and a dull yellow colour like brass.

When it saw Theseus, it rushed upon him, bellowing with rage and hunger. Theseus, of course, had no weapon: but as the creature came he smote it over the heart with his fist, and then leapt aside. Bellowing more fiercely than ever, the Minotaur came at him again; and again he smote, and sprang aside. Again and again he did this, until at last the creature began to weaken. Finally Theseus seized it by the horns and forced back its head, back and back until with a mighty crack the neck broke, and the Minotaur lay dead.

After resting a little, Theseus picked up the end of his clue, and began to follow it back, winding it up as he went. In this way he at length reached the door, where Ariadne was waiting for him. Swiftly she led him and the other intended victims to their ship; and while it was still dark they crept on board, cut the cables, and stole silently away.

They sailed over the sea towards Athens, and on the way stopped to rest on the lovely island of Naxos. This, as it happened, was specially dear to Dionysus; and there he and the Satyrs were feasting and making merry at this time. Dionysus saw Ariadne as she wandered through the leafy woods, and fell in love with her dark, wild beauty. So he cast her into a magic sleep, as he so easily could by turning a spring or a stream into wine; and when she awoke, she remembered nothing about Theseus, nor how she came to Naxos, but willingly became the bride of Dionysus.

Theseus, meanwhile, searched the island for her in vain, and at last sailed sadly away, mourning the princess who had saved him. And he was still so lost in melancholy that as he sailed up the Gulf of Aegina and drew near to Athens, he forgot to hang white sails from his mast in place of black, and Aegeus watching for him believed that his son was dead, and cast himself down from the rock of the acropolis, and so died.

In his memory the sea between Greece and Asia Minor is called the Aegean to this very day.

Minos did not pursue Theseus and Ariadne: instead, he set out in search of Daedalus the clever craftsman who had made the Labyrinth and sworn that no man could ever find his way out of it.

For Daedalus, as soon as he learnt that Theseus had escaped, fled from Crete, knowing that Minos would seek to punish him. No ship would take him, but Daedalus made wings out of feathers fastened together with wax for himself and his son Icarus.

'Do not go too high,' cautioned Daedalus as they set out. But Icarus, overbold when he found how well he could fly, went too near to the sun. Then the wax melted from his wings and he fell into the sea, which was ever afterwards called the Icarian, and was drowned.

But Daedalus reached land in safety, and no one knew

where he had gone. Minos, however, was cunning and the way he set about his quest was this: he carried with him a spiral shell, and gave out that whoever could thread a piece of silk through it should have a vast reward. He felt certain that no one but Daedalus was clever enough to perform this seemingly impossible feat.

His guess proved correct, for when he came to Sicily, King Cocalus took the shell and brought it back next morning with the thread drawn through it.

'Daedalus is here!' exclaimed Minos, and threatened a terrible vengeance unless he was given up to him.

'You are right,' confessed Cocalus. 'He indeed threaded the shell. He fastened the silk to the hind leg of an ant and allowed it to crawl through the spiral, drawing the thread after it. I will certainly give him up to you, tomorrow. But tonight come and feast with us.'

Suspecting nothing, Minos agreed readily. But that night as he lay in his bath, the Princess of Sicily who had fallen in love with Daedalus, poured boiling water down a pipe which the master craftsman had prepared, and Minos was scalded to death.

Meanwhile Theseus had become King of Athens, and when he heard that Minos was dead, he made peace with the new king of Crete, who sent him his sister Phaedra in marriage, so that, in spite of his loss of Ariadne, he still married a daughter of Minos.

Then he ruled in Athens for some time, bringing peace

and order to the country; though he was careful to kill any of his cousins whom he could catch, in case they should try to seize the throne.

In time he grew weary of his peaceful life, and longed for further adventures. So he was overjoyed when a message reached him from a young Prince called Jason urging him to join an expedition in search of the Golden Fleece from the Ram which carried Phrixus and Helle over the sea from Greece many years before.

Eagerly Theseus set out for Iolcus, where Jason was gathering a band of Heroes for his quest, among whom the most famous was Heracles himself – free from his servitude at last and longing for a real adventure after the years as a slave to Queen Omphale.

CHAPTER FIFTEEN

THE QUEST OF THE GOLDEN FLEECE

Then Jason said: 'A happy lot is mine!
Surely the gods must love me, since that thou
Art come, with me the rough green plain to
  plough
That no man reaps; yet certes, thou alone
In after days shall be the glorious one
Whom men shall sing of when they name the
  Fleece,
That bore the son of Athamas from Greece!'

WILLIAM MORRIS
The Life and Death of Jason

15

Jason's father was the rightful king of Iolcus, but he was deposed by his brother Pelias, the father of Alcestis, who tried to murder the true heir. Jason, however, was smuggled away to the Centaur Chiron, who tended him carefully in his mountain cave and trained him in all things suiting a prince.

Pelias, meanwhile, reigned in Iolcus – though not very happily, since an oracle had told him to 'beware of the man with a single sandal', who would cause his death.

When Jason was grown up, he set out for Iolcus to seek his fortune there, and also to find his father and see if he could come to some agreement with his wicked uncle. On the way he came to a ford through the river Anaurus, where the flood-water was running swiftly. An old woman sitting on the bank cried out when she saw Jason:

'Good sir, will you carry me across; for you are young and strong, with mighty things before you: but I am too old and feeble to battle with the waters of this river.'

'Certainly I will, good mother!' said Jason kindly, and he lifted the old woman on to his shoulders and entered the stream. It was a difficult crossing, and Jason was almost exhausted when he struggled up the further bank, and he had lost one sandal in the mud of the river's bed.

He set down his ancient burden – and then fell on his knees with amazement and awe. For instead of the old woman, the tall and stately form of a shining Immortal stood before him.

'Do not be afraid, Jason,' she said. 'I am Hera, Queen of Heaven, and your friend. Go forward as you are, and speak the words that I shall put into your mouth, and you will become one of the most famous Heroes in all Greece!'

Then she vanished, and Jason went on his way rejoicing, and came to Iolcus in the evening, when Pelias was holding a great feast.

'*The man with one sandal!*' Pelias turned pale and trembled when he saw. And when he learnt that this was his nephew, the rightful heir to the throne, he grew even more afraid. But he hid his fear and his hatred, and welcomed Jason warmly.

'I need just such a man to be my counsellor,' he said heartily. 'And to test your wisdom, let me ask you what, supposing you had the power, you would do if you received an oracle that you were to be deposed by a certain one of your subjects?'

'Do?' exclaimed Jason. 'I would command him to bring home the Golden Fleece from Colchis!'

'Excellent advice!' cried Pelias gleefully. 'You are yourself the man, and you must perform this quest!'

'I will indeed,' said Jason quietly. 'And on my return, I shall fulfil the oracle!'

'I shall yield up the throne to you willingly,' said Pelias, '*when* you return with the Golden Fleece!'

Jason sought the help of Argus, a skilled ship-builder who, with the aid of Athena, made a ship of fifty oars named *Argo* after its maker; and Athena fastened to its prow a magic branch from the oak-tree of Dodona which on occasion could speak, prophesying the future or offering advice.

Next Jason sent heralds throughout Greece calling on the bravest of the young kings and princes to join him on the quest and win immortal fame. From all parts they came trooping to Iolcus – and their names were the names of Heroes still remembered, and their children were the Heroes who fought at Troy.

First came Heracles, with Hylas his esquire; and then Theseus from Athens, and young Castor and Polydeuces from Sparta, with their wild cousins Idas and Lyceus. Telamon came, and Peleus, who had been the companions of Heracles on his expedition against the Amazons; and the wondrous sons of the North Wind, Zetes and Calais, who had wings growing from their shoulders. Admetus came, and Oileus; Laertes the father of Odysseus; Meleager whose strange tale is yet to be told, and Atalanta the Maiden Huntress, the follower of Artemis; Nestor, the only Argonaut to fight at Troy, and many another whose names are recorded in the old books.

There came also the divine singer, Orpheus, the son of Apollo. When he played upon his lyre and sang sweetly the wild beasts followed him in friendship, and the very trees and flowers bowed to the power of his music. But his heart was filled with sadness, for his wife Eurydice had been bitten by a snake and died. Orpheus followed her to the Land of the Dead, and at the wonder of his music, Charon ferried him across the black River Styx and Cerberus let him pass: even Hades was overcome and gave him back his lost Eurydice – but on condition that he did not look behind to see if she was following, until they stood again in the sunlight. But Orpheus, fearing lest Charon had refused to take her across the Styx, looked back once – and Eurydice was lost to him for ever.

When the Heroes were gathered at Iolcus, they hung

their shields upon the rails of the *Argo*, and set sail over the dancing waves, while Orpheus played to them, and Tiphys the skilled helmsman guided the ship.

Northwards they sailed, and came to the land of King Cyzicus, who entertained them kindly. When they put to sea again, a great storm took the ship and whirled it around in the darkness till they came to a shore that they did not know, and the inhabitants took them for pirates and attacked them in the night.

Fiercely the battle raged, and the Argonauts (as those who sailed in the *Argo* were called) proved victorious. But what was their grief and horror to find when the day dawned that it was the land of kind King Cyzicus to which they had returned without knowing, and that he and many of his warriors lay dead at their hands.

Sorrowing deeply, they sailed north again, and came to Mysia, not far from Troy, and here Heracles was left behind. For young Hylas went to draw water from a deep pool, and the water-nymphs who dwelt in it fell in love with him and drew him down into the depths to live there with them for ever. Heracles searched for him far and wide, and a great wind rising drove the *Argo* out to sea, so that he was forced to make his way to Colchis over land.

Next the Argonauts visited King Amycus who challenged his guests to a boxing match, and killed each in turn. This time he was met in the ring by Polydeuces, who smote him so hard that he fell to the ground and died.

Sailing onwards they landed in Thrace where the blind King Phineus dwelt, a seer nevertheless, who could look through distance.

'Help us,' they begged, 'and tell us what things to do and what to avoid on our way to Colchis.'

'Help you I will,' said Phineus, 'if you first free me from the Harpies!' Then he set a feast before them: but scarcely had they tasted it when down came the two Harpies – terrible winged women with great claws – who carried off the best of the food, and made the rest uneatable.

Then Zetes and Calais, the winged sons of the North Wind, drew their swords and leapt into the air in pursuit of them, and neither were seen again, though the Harpies never more visited King Phineus.

Now fully instructed as to their way, the Argonauts sailed up the Hellespont and came to the Clashing Rocks which guarded the entrance to the Black Sea. These were great floating masses of blue rock which crashed together and crushed any ship which tried to pass them.

Following King Phineus's advice, Jason let loose a heron, and followed it until they drew near to the Rocks, which were half veiled in mist and spray.

Presently the bird sped between them: the Rocks crashed together, just touching her tail, and then rebounded on either side.

Immediately Tiphys guided the *Argo* through the gap, while every hero strained at his oar. The ship shot between the Rocks, which clashed together only in time to nip the ornament from the end of the stern. From this time on the Clashing Rocks stood still, for it was fated that once a ship had passed them in safety, they could move no more.

The Argonauts sailed on, into the Black Sea, and along its southern coast, until they came to the River Phasis at its eastern end – the river that still runs red down from the Caucasus in memory of the blood which Prometheus shed there for mankind.

Up the river they went, and came to the city of Colchis where Aeetes was king, the fierce son of Helios, whose sister Circe and his daughter Medea were skilled in the black art of witchcraft.

'I will give you the Golden Fleece,' said King Aeetes when Jason told him of their quest, 'if you can yoke my brazen-footed bulls which breathe fire from their nostrils, plough a field with them, and sow it with dragons' teeth!'

That night Jason sat wondering sadly how he was to accomplish this task: for not even Heracles, who had rejoined the Argonauts, could have accomplished it. Then Medea the Witch-Maiden came to him, and said:

'I will tell you how to do this thing, and how to take the Fleece, if you will promise to let me sail back to Greece with you and there become your wife.'

This Jason swore to do, though he had little liking for

witches and witchcraft: and Medea instructed him, and gave him a magic ointment which would make him invulnerable and unburnable for a single day.

In the morning, Jason anointed himself with the ointment and to the amazement of King Aeetes harnessed the bulls without taking any harm. He ploughed the field, and afterwards sowed it with dragons' teeth. But the moment they were sown, the teeth began to grow: and the crop was not corn, but armed men all eager for war and ready to slay Jason.

But Jason remembered what Medea had told him, and flung the helmet which had held the dragons' teeth into the midst of the armed men. At once they began to fight fiercely among themselves, and before long they all lay dead.

'Tomorrow you shall have the Golden Fleece,' promised Aeetes: but before then he plotted to burn the *Argo* and murder the Argonauts.

Medea again came to Jason, and warned him, and in the night she led him and Orpheus to the magic garden where the Golden Fleece hung on the Tree at the World's End, guarded by a dragon – just as the Apples of the Hesperides hung in their garden at the World's opposite end.

It was a dim, mysterious place, high-walled and pillared with the dark boles of mighty trees. Through the dappling moonlight Medea the Witch-Maiden led the way, until they came to the centre where the Golden Fleece shone in the darkness as it hung from a tree round which coiled a dragon larger and more terrible than any in the world.

'Play and sing!' whispered Medea to Orpheus, and she began to murmur a spell while he touched gently on the strings of his lyre and sang in a sweet low voice his Hymn to Sleep:

> 'Sleep, king of gods and men,
>   Master of all;
> Come to mine eyes again,
>   Come as I call!
> Sleep, who may loose and bind
>   Each as his thrall,
> Come to the weary mind,
>   Come at my call!
> Tamer of toil and woes,
>   Healer of all;
> Sleep, whence our solace flows,
>   Come as I call!
> Brother of all mankind,
>   Softly you fall
> Leaving the world behind:
>   Come at my call!
> Sleep, lord of all things made,
>   Sleep over all
> Let your warm wings be laid,
>   Come as I call!'

As Orpheus sang it seemed that the very garden slept: the wind grew still; the flowers drooped their heads, and not a leaf stirred. The great gleaming dragon slid slowly from the tree, coil within coil, and, resting its terrible head on a bank of sleeping red poppies, slept for the first and last time in its life.

Only by the charms of Medea did Jason himself remain awake, and when he saw that the dragon slept, he drew near and looked up at the shining Fleece.

Then Medea sprinkled the dragon with her magic brew, and whispered to Jason:

'Climb! Climb swiftly up the coils of its back and take down the Fleece, for my charms will not hold it long!'

So Jason, not without dread, mounted that terrible ladder into the great ilex-tree and unhooked the Golden Fleece which had hung there ever since Phrixus stripped it from the magic Ram; and by its light he found his way through the garden.

For Medea, by her charms, called for Hecate, the Immortal Queen of the Witches, and by her help the moon was darkened, and night closed over Colchis like a black cloak.

Going swiftly by secret paths, they came to the river's edge where the *Argo* lay ready, and they stepped on board, Medea taking with her the young Prince Absyrtus, her brother. Then the Argonauts bent to their oars, and rowed so mightily that the stout pine, hewn on Mount Pelion, bent like withies of hazel in their hands as they sped towards the sea.

But suddenly in the darkness behind them the Dragon woke from its charmed sleep, and found that the Golden Fleece had gone. Then it uttered its terrible voice, a hissing and a groaning cry so fearful that all the people of Colchis woke at the sound and the women clutched their children to them and shivered with fear.

King Aeetes, however, guessed what had happened and, dark though it was, launched a swift ship and set off in pursuit of the Argonauts.

'Row! Row!' cried Medea, when she heard the Dragon's cry. 'My father's ships are very swift, and there will be no mercy for any of us if we are taken!'

So they bent to their oars again, and the water was churned into foam as they sped down the Phasis and came with the dawning out into the Black Sea and away to the west.

Before noon they saw the tall ship of King Aeetes drawing up behind them, and in the dim distance others of the Colchian fleet coming in pursuit.

In vain Orpheus played on his lyre to cheer them as they laboured at the oars; and in vain did the winds fill the *Argo*'s sail. The great ships of Colchis drew nearer, ever nearer.

Then Medea the Witch did a dreadful thing, while the Argonauts looked on in horror, but dared do nothing because it was she who had saved them, and Jason had sworn to marry her and bring her unhurt to Greece.

She took her brother, the boy prince Absyrtus and killed him with a sharp sword in plain view of his father, King Aeetes. Then she cut him in pieces and cast the pieces into the sea, for she knew that Aeetes would stop to gather them up so as to give his son due and honourable burial – without which, so they believed, his ghost could find no rest in the Realm of Hades or in the Fields of Elysium.

All happened as she expected. King Aeetes, standing weeping at the prow of his ship, uttered a terrible curse upon Medea and upon all who sailed in the *Argo*; then he halted his fleet to gather up the remains of his son, and the Argonauts sailed on and were lost to view in the wide sea; nor did Aeetes and his fleet find them again.

But Jason bowed his head with shame and misery: for what Medea had done was terrible and not to be forgiven; but now he was bound to her, and had married a Witch who would bring him no good fortune in the end.

CHAPTER SIXTEEN

THE RETURN OF THE ARGONAUTS

Forth from thy father's home
  Thou camest, O heart of fire,
To the Dark Blue Rocks, to the clashing foam,
  To the seas of thy desire:

Till the Dark Blue Bar was crossed;
  And lo, by an alien river
Standing, thy lover lost,
  Void-armed for ever.

EURIPIDES
Medea (Translated by Gilbert Murray)

16

Under the dark shadow of Medea's crime, the Argonauts sailed away into the mysterious distance to the north and west of the Black Sea, and presently a storm overtook the ship, spun it round, and carried it through the darkness, no one knew whither. But, as they were driven between islands and the high cliffs of what might be a great river's mouth, the Magic Branch of Dodona set at the prow spoke to them:

'You who have sinned so deeply cannot escape the wrath of Zeus, nor come to your native land again, until you have visited the Island of Aeaea: for Circe the Enchantress alone can purify you. But the way thither is long and terrible such as no man has sailed before.'

The Argonauts cried out with fear at that eerie voice; then the wind took them again, and darkness closed about them, and they sailed on and on, they knew not where nor whither.

On and ever on they went, sometimes rowing and sometimes blown by the wind; and Orpheus played upon his lyre. Up the river, up and up into the cold north they went; and at length, rowing against the stream until it grew too shallow for them, they landed and carried the *Argo* on their shoulders.

Of that terrible journey little has been told, nor could any of the Argonauts say for certain where they went. But when they were ready to die with weariness, they came to another river flowing north-west and floated down it to a sea where the sun was dimmed by mists, and icicles gathered and hung from the mast and the spars of the *Argo*, and when they landed they saw great white bears.

There were also wild men in those parts; the Laestrygonians, who wore skins and fought with battle-axes, singing wild songs of Odin and the halls of Valhalla, and they foamed at the mouth with berserk rage while they fought.

Shivering with cold, the Argonauts rowed quickly past these frozen coasts where the sun shone at midnight, but did not warm them even at midday. They came then into the Northern Sea and past the land beyond the North Wind, the Ultimate Islands, which in later days were called Britain. Still on they sailed into the Western Ocean where it was said that the Land of Atlantis had sunk beneath the waters not long before; and then south across a stormy bay until at last the sun grew warmer, and one day Heracles cried:

'My friends, we have come back to the known world again! Over yonder stand the two pillars which I set up to mark the entrance to Our Sea, and to the southward Titan Atlas holds up the heavens upon his mountain peak while below is the Garden of the Hesperides!'

He told them of his quest for the Golden Apples, and they marvelled at all he had seen and done. They marvelled still more when he led them to the Garden itself: for there lay the Serpent Ladon, the tip of its tail moving, though it was fifteen years since Heracles had slain it with his poisoned arrow.

The Argonauts rested in that fragrant land until their strength and health came back to them; and they raised altars and sacrificed to the Immortals in gratitude for bringing them safely through such dangers.

Then they sailed on once more, over the blue Mediterranean Sea, passing between Corsica and Sardinia, and came to Aeaea, the little island where dwelt Medea's aunt, the enchantress Circe.

Now if they had come alone, Circe would have worked

some evil enchantment upon the Argonauts, but when she saw Medea she hastened to make them welcome. And when Medea told of her crime and the command of Zeus, spoken by the magic bough, she purified them all of the blood of Absyrtus, and sent them on their way with a load lifted from their hearts.

But their adventures were not yet ended. Near to Aeaea was another island, which is now called Capri, and on it lived the Sirens. These were once maidens who had played with Persephone the Divine Maiden in that fair field of Enna in Sicily from which Hades carried her away to be Queen of the Dead. They had prayed to have wings so as to go through the world in search of her, and Demeter granted their wish. But in some strange way they turned to evil, and so were doomed to live on their beautiful island and lure sailors to their death. They still had wings, but they had the claws and tails of birds also, and they sang so sweetly that no man who heard could resist their singing. For whoever heard that wonderful song forgot all else, plunged into the waves, and swam to shore: and there the Sirens would catch him with their sharp claws, and tear him to pieces. But it was fated that if anyone could resist their singing and sail away unhurt, then the Sirens would meet their end.

When the Argonauts drew near and heard the wondrous song of the Sirens, they bent eagerly to their oars, longing only to land on that island and listen to the enchantment of their singing. But Medea knew what fate lay in store for any who set foot on the Isle of the Sirens, and she cried to Orpheus:

'Divine musician, play on your lyre and sing for our lives! Surely you, the son of Apollo, can sing even more sweetly than these creatures of beauty and evil!'

Orpheus played as never before, and sang such a strain as that which had ravished the ears of Hades and drawn his lost Eurydice from the dead. And the Argonauts listened to his singing, and forgot the Sirens, and were able to turn the ship from that fatal island and sail for the south. All, that is, except Butes, who sprang into the sea and swam towards the Sirens: but Aphrodite took pity on him, and carried him away in time, to become a priest at her shrine in the south of Sicily.

As for the Sirens, as mortal men had withstood their song, Fate came upon them and, like the Sphinx when Oedipus solved her riddle, they flung themselves down from their rock and died. All except two, who had not joined in the song that day, and so lived to sing still, to lure sailors to their doom until Odysseus passed that way on his return from Troy.

On sailed the Argonauts, seeing many other wonders. They passed the cave where lurked Scylla the many-headed monster; though on that day she slept. They passed the whirlpool of Charybdis in safety, and the Floating Islands which flung out burning rocks, and the Island where

Helios, the Sun Titan, kept his milk-white kine with horns of gold, and the happy land of the Phaeacians.

Here they tarried a while, and the wedding of Jason and Medea was celebrated. For while they rested in Phaeacia the ships of King Aeetes arrived, and the Phaeacian King said that while he was ready to give up the daughter of Aeetes, he would defend the wife of Jason! So the Colchians failed of their design, and as Aeetes had sworn to slay them all if they returned without Medea, they settled down and formed a new kingdom of their own next door to Phaeacia.

The *Argo* sailed again soon after the wedding, and a storm took it as it rounded Cape Malea at the south of Greece, and drove it across the sea to Crete.

Now in the early days the Smith of the Immortals, Hephaestus, had fashioned for the first King Minos a man of brass called Talos, a giant who ran round the island three times in every day and sank any ship which drew near, by hurling great stones on it.

Minos knew how to control this monster, as did all the Kings of Crete until the last Minos had sailed away in pursuit of Daedalus after Theseus killed the Minotaur and escaped from the Labyrinth. But Deucalion, the new King, did not know how to deal with Talos, and he himself had escaped with difficulty from Crete to join the Argonauts and sail with Jason.

The monster Talos was now quite out of control, and Crete was cut off by him from the outer world, for he still ran round the island three times a day, pelting any ship which drew near. At other times he made himself red hot by lying in a bath of fire, and then burned up all that he touched.

Deucalion now begged the other Argonauts to help him to destroy Talos, but not even Heracles could think how to do it.

Then Medea said: 'Only with the help of magic, and by great guile can we overcome Talos. But do just as I say, and all will be well.'

So when she had instructed them, they drew near to the island, and presently Talos appeared, glowing red with heat, a great rock ready in his hands.

Then first of all Orpheus played his sweetest strains, so that Talos paused, uncertain, while Medea spoke to him:

'Noble Talos,' said she, 'I am Medea the Witch, and I can make you King of the World, and ruler even over the Immortals, if you will make me your Queen.'

'How can you do that?' rumbled the giant doubtfully.

'Is it not true,' asked Medea, 'that you have but one vein in your body, running from neck to heel, and that instead of blood it contains ichor, the immortal liquid which flows in the veins of the Immortals?'

Talos nodded doubtfully, and Medea went on: 'Although ichor flows in your vein, you are not immortal: but I, by my magic arts, can make you so, if you will let me land safely with one follower.'

Talos agreed to this, and Medea landed, with Poeas who was the smallest man among the Argonauts. If Heracles or Theseus had tried to step ashore, Talos might have suspected some plot, but little Poeas could arouse nobody's suspicion and Talos did not know that he was one of the most skilful archers living – nor that Heracles had lent him his bow and arrows.

Once on the shore, Poeas wandered away and settled himself quietly out of sight among the rocks. But Medea took a sickle with a blade of brass and began to gather herbs with which to make a magic brew. She mixed them in a cauldron, squeezing the milk-white juices from them, and singing an incantation. Next she stripped off her clothes, bound up her jet-black hair with wreaths of ivy, and bent over the cauldron, chopping the herbs and roots and singing wildly.

Talos was fascinated by the lovely Witch-wife and her magic brew; he drew nearer and nearer, but still mistrustfully. For in his heel was set a brass nail, like a stopper, which prevented the ichor from escaping, and he feared greatly lest anyone should touch it.

Medea had soon brewed her magic draught, and now she held it out to Talos in a cup: 'Drink!' she said. 'It is the wine of Immortality!'

And Talos was so bewitched that he took the cup and drained it. But it brought to him only a great drowsiness so that presently he was reeling about as if drunken, but still determined not to fall asleep lest anyone should draw out the nail.

Then Poeas rose, fitted an arrow to the bow, and shot with such skill that the arrow struck the nail in Talos's heel and loosened it so that it fell to the ground and the ichor gushed out.

At this Talos cried aloud and groped for the nail: but the magic brew was too strong for him, and he could not find it, and presently he lay cold and still – an image of brass, nothing more.

After this the Argonauts landed in Crete and were entertained lavishly by Deucalion before setting sail for Iolcus, which they reached without further adventures.

There they parted, though very soon a number of them met again for the adventure of the Calydonian Boar which, at his homecoming, Meleager found was ravaging his land.

Jason did not live to enjoy the old age of honour which was his due. He died childless and alone, with the curse of Aeetes upon him, for there was no purification which could free him wholly from the guilt of Absyrtus's murder.

When he returned to Iolcus he found his old father was dead, and Pelias still ruling there. Jason was content to let him remain as king for the rest of his life, but Medea the Witch wished to be queen. So while Jason was away at Calydon she said to the daughters of Pelias: 'You know my magic powers: would you like to learn from me how to make your father young again?'

At first they mistrusted her. So Medea mixed a magic brew in a great cauldron; and she took an old ram, so old it could hardly walk. She killed it, cut it into small pieces, and threw them into the cauldron. And at once there leapt out of it a young lamb, strong and bold and frisky.

Then the daughters of Pelias doubted her no longer. They took their old father, killed him and cut him up. But when they placed the pieces in the cauldron, Pelias remained as dead as ever – for Medea had not taught them her evil spell.

But when the people of Iolcus discovered what Medea had done, they banished her and Jason, who wandered away to Corinth. There Jason had a chance of a new kingdom: for the king had only one child, the maiden Glauce.

'You shall marry her and rule this land,' said the king, 'if you will send away that evil Witch, Medea.'

Jason, who had never loved Medea, and by now hated her for her cruelty and wickedness, consented to this, and Medea appeared to agree, but she gave Glauce a magic wedding dress which burned her to death the moment she put it on, and burned her father also who tried to save her.

Then Medea killed her own and Jason's two sons, and fled away in a chariot drawn by flying dragons.

But Jason became an outcast, and in his wanderings he returned to where the old ship *Argo* was drawn up on the beach.

'You are my only friend,' he said sadly as he sat down to rest in the shade of the ship. There he fell asleep, and while he slept the front of the ship, grown rotten with age, fell suddenly on his head and killed him.

CHAPTER SEVENTEEN

Meleager and Atalanta

The maid has vowed e'en such a man to wed
As in the course her swift feet can outrun,
But whoso fails herein, his days are done . . .
   Behold, such mercy Atalanta gives
To those that long to win her loveliness.

WILLIAM MORRIS
The Earthly Paradise

17

Meleager the Argonaut bore a charmed life. For when he was but seven days old the Three Fates appeared to his mother Queen Althaea of Calydon as she lay in the big shadowy room of the palace lit only by the flickering fire-light.

The Fates were the three daughters of Zeus and Themis who presided over the fate of man: and when Althaea saw them, they were busy with the life-thread of her son Meleager.

One Fate spun the thread of life, and that was Clotho, and she was spinning busily, while Lachesis stood by with her rod to measure it. The third Fate, Atropos, held the shears, and she said to her sisters:

'Why trouble you to spin and measure? As soon as that brand on the hearth yonder is consumed to ashes, I must cut the thread with my shears, and Meleager's life will be ended!'

When Althaea heard this, she leapt out of bed, snatched the burning brand from the hearth and put out the flames. Then she hid it away in a secret chest of which she alone possessed the key.

'Now I defy you, Fates!' she cried. 'I have but to preserve that brand, and my son will live for ever!'

Then the Three Sisters smiled at Althaea, and there was a secret knowledge in their eyes which made her afraid. After that, they vanished and only the charred brand in her secret chest remained to prove that she had not dreamed it all.

Years passed and Meleager grew into a brave young prince and went with Jason and the other Argonauts in quest of the Golden Fleece. On his return to Calydon he found a savage wild boar ravaging the land, destroying all the crops and killing any who tried to withstand it.

This great Boar, with its wonderful tusks and hide, was not to be slain by one man, and Meleager sent for his friends among the Argonauts, Heracles and Theseus, Peleus and Telamon, Admetus, and Nestor, Jason himself, and several others – but in particular he sent for the maiden huntress Atalanta. For Meleager had fallen in love with her during their voyage on the *Argo*, and still hoped to persuade her to be his wife, though she had sworn never to marry.

Atalanta was a princess of Arcadia, but when she was born her father King Iasus of Tegea, disappointed that she was not a boy, had cast her out on to the wild mountain side. Here a she-bear found the baby and brought her up among her own cubs; and Artemis, the Immortal Huntress, trained her in all matters of the chase and allowed her to join with the nymphs who were her followers.

Now she came eagerly to Calydon, and was welcomed by Meleager and the other Argonauts. But Phexippus and Toxeus, Meleager's uncles, the beloved brothers of Queen Althaea, protested when they saw Atalanta.

'It is an insult,' they cried, 'to expect us to go hunting in company with a woman! She should be weaving at her loom, not mixing with men and pretending to skill in the chase!'

Meleager angrily bade them be silent, and the hunt began, with Atalanta walking at his side – a lovely maiden, simple and boyish, with hair falling to her shoulders, a tunic of skins, and a long bow in her hand.

'How happy will the man be who can call himself your husband!' sighed Meleager.

Atalanta blushed and frowned, saying: 'Never by my

free will shall any man do so . . . But let us give all our thoughts to this fierce Boar which we seek.'

They had not far to go, for in a wooded dell overhung by willows and dense with smooth sedge and marshy rushes, the Boar was roused. Out he came in a fury, levelling the young trees and bushes as he went, and scattering the dogs to right and left.

Echion flung a spear, but in his eagerness pinned only the trunk of a maple-tree. Jason hurled his weapon, but it too passed over the Boar's back. Squealing with rage, while his eyes flashed fire, it rushed upon young Nestor – who would never have lived to fight at Troy if he had not swung himself quickly into a tree out of harm's way.

Then Telamon rushed at the Boar with his spear ready, but he tripped over an unseen root, and was barely rescued by Peleus. As he staggered to his feet, the Boar charged: and it would have gone hard with them both if Atalanta had not, with quiet skill and courage, drawn her bow-string and sent an arrow whizzing into the Boar's head close to its ear. Yet even her skill could not send an arrow right to the brain, so hard was the creature's skin.

There was no one so delighted as Meleager: 'See!' he cried, 'the Princess Atalanta has taught us men how to hunt boars, and has smitten the creature with a mortal wound!'

Ancaeus, who had also objected to a woman joining in

the hunt, was furious at this. 'Watch!' he cried, 'I'll show you how a man settles wild boars! No pin-pricks from a woman will do it. A battle axe is the weapon, and Artemis herself could not defend this Boar against me!'

So saying, he rushed at the maddened creature and struck – but struck short. The next moment he was on his back, and the Boar had killed him. In an effort to save him, Peleus flung his spear: but Eurytion sprang forward at the same moment with his weapon raised, and the spear meant for the Boar passed through his body.

Theseus also launched a spear, but aimed high in his excitement and transfixed only the bough of an oak-tree. But Meleager's aim was true, and the Boar fell to the ground, and he dispatched it with a blow of his second spear.

Then the hunters shouted with joy, and stood around gazing in awe at the great creature covering so large a patch of ground. Meleager knelt down and set to work skinning the Boar, and when he had done so, he turned to Atalanta and presented her with the head and hide.

'Lady,' he said, 'take the spoils and share my glory with me. You were the first to wound the Boar and more honour belongs to you than to me or any other one of us.'

Then the rest envied Atalanta her prize, and Phexippus, Meleager's uncle, could not contain his fury:

'This is the worst insult of all!' he shouted. 'My nephew won the skin, and if he did not want it, he should have given it to me, as the most noble person present! As for you, you shameless girl, do not think that we will suffer this dishonour. You may have bewitched Meleager with your beauty, but it has no power on us!'

At that he and his brother Toxeus seized hold of Atalanta and tore the spoils from her as roughly and insultingly as they could.

Then Meleager lost his temper completely. With a yell of rage he drew his sword and stabbed Phexippus to the heart. Then he turned upon Toxeus, who tried to defend himself, but soon lay dead beside his brother. Then the party set out sadly for the city, carrying the dead bodies with them, while Atalanta held the head and hide of the Calydonian Boar.

When Queen Althaea saw that her two brothers were dead, her grief knew no bounds. But when she learnt that Meleager had killed them, her grief turned to a wild frenzy of fury and revenge.

Suddenly she remembered the charred brand which she had snatched from the hearth when Meleager was a baby. Rushing to her room, she drew it from the chest and cast it upon the fire, where it caught quickly, flamed up, and was soon reduced to ashes.

Now Meleager was feasting his friends in the hall and drinking the health of Atalanta. All at once the cup fell from his hand, and with a cry he sank to the ground, writhing there in agony. He cried out that he was burning from within, and that he wished the Boar had killed him instead of Ancaeus; and in a few minutes he lay dead.

Then there was mourning throughout Calydon, and the great Boar Hunt which had begun so happily ended in sadness and tragedy. Queen Althaea, when she came to herself after her frenzy of grief and rage, was so horrified at what she had done that she hanged herself.

But one happy result came of the Calydonian Boar hunt, for Heracles fell in love with Meleager's sister, the Princess Deianira. Now King Oeneus had promised her, against her will, to the River Achelous, who came to him in the shape of a fierce man and threatened to destroy his land if he refused his suit.

When Heracles heard this, he went to the river bank and cried: 'Noble River Achelous, we both love the same maiden! Come forth, then, in whatever form you choose, and fight with me for her!'

Achelous accepted this daring challenge, took the form of a great, savage bull, and charged at Heracles. But that mighty Hero was experienced by now in such contests, and seizing Achelous by one horn he snapped it off at the root. Then Achelous submitted, and Deianira became the wife of Heracles, and they lived happily for a while at Calydon, helping Oeneus until his young son Tydeus should be old enough to rule.

The other hunters had, meanwhile, returned to their homes; but the beautiful Atalanta, famous now for her part in the battle with the Boar, was claimed by her father, King Iasus.

She settled at his home, not far from Calydon, but still refused to marry.

'But I have no son to succeed me!' lamented Iasus. 'Choose whom you will as husband, and you shall rule here jointly, and your children after you.'

'I will obey you, as a daughter should,' said Atalanta at length. 'But on one condition. Every prince who comes as my suitor must race with me. Only he that is swifter of foot than I, shall be my husband. But, those whom I beat in the race shall forfeit their lives.'

Iasus was forced to agree, and sent heralds throughout Greece proclaiming that whoever could outrun his daughter Atalanta should marry her and be king of Tegea; but that those who lost the race would lose their heads also.

Several princes felt confident that they could run faster than any girl, and came to try their fortune. But each of them in turn left his head to decorate the finishing-post on King Iasus's race course.

Soon no one else dared to try, and Atlanta smiled happily for she was determined never to marry.

At length her cousin Prince Melanion fell in love with her and knowing that he could not surpass her in running, he prayed to Aphrodite, the Immortal Queen of Love and Beauty, to assist him.

Aphrodite was angry with Atalanta for scorning love and refusing to marry, and she granted Melanion her help. She lent him the three Golden Apples which Heracles had brought from the Garden of the Hesperides, and which Athena had passed on to her for this very purpose.

Then Melanion presented himself in Tegea, and in spite of all King Iasus's warnings, insisted on racing for Atalanta.

The course was set, and the race began. At first Atalanta let Melanion gain on her, for she knew that she was twice as fast a runner as he was. When he saw her shadow drawing close to him, he dropped a golden apple which rolled in front of her.

Atalanta saw the apple, and was filled with the desire to possess this wonderful thing. So she stopped quickly, picked it up and then sped after Melanion, certain of overtaking him easily. And so she did, but as she drew level, he dropped a second apple, and again she could not resist the temptation, but stopped and picked it up.

Once more she sped after Melanion, and once more she overtook him. But a third apple rolled across in front of her, and at the sight of its beauty and wonder, Atalanta forgot all else, and stopped to gather it.

'I can still overtake him!' she thought, and sped on like the wind. But Melanion touched the winning-post a moment before she reached him, and so he won her for his wife. And in a little while they were living happily together as king and queen of Tegea, with a small son to be king after them.

Heracles and Deianira were happy too, living quietly at Calydon, though in time they were forced to move again, as Heracles in a quarrel struck a cousin of the king's so hard that he died. So they bade farewell to Oeneus and set out on their travels towards the north of Greece.

Now, on their way, they came to the river Evenus where lived the Centaur called Nessus who hated Heracles. This Centaur was accustomed to carry travellers across the river on his back; and when he had taken Deianira nearly to the other side, he suddenly turned down stream, and began to carry her away. She screamed for help, and Heracles drew his bow and shot Nessus with one of his poisoned arrows.

As he lay dying on the river bank, Nessus gasped:

Lady Deianira, I will tell you a secret. When I am dead keep a little of the blood from my wound, and if ever you find that Heracles has ceased to love you, soak a robe in it and give it him to wear: that will make him love you more than ever before.'

Then he died, and Deianira did as she was instructed, believing that Nessus had told her this to show how sorry he was for what he had tried to do. But she did not tell Heracles.

After this they came safely to Trachis, a hundred miles

north of Thebes, and were welcomed by King Ceyx. And there they settled down safely and happily.

But for Heracles there was never to be any real peace or rest, and indeed he did not wish it, for very soon he set out on a new and dangerous expedition.

CHAPTER EIGHTEEN

THE FIRST FALL OF TROY

Where Heracles wandered, the lonely
   Bow-bearer, he lent him his hands
For the wrecking of one land only,
Of Ilion, Ilion only,
    Most hated of lands!

EURIPIDES
Trojan Women (Translated by Gilbert Murray)

18

Whe hen Heracles rescued Hesione, daughter of the
King of Troy, from the sea monster, he was not
able to take the reward with him, as he was still labouring
for Eurystheus of Tiryns. But when his labours were ended,
he sent to King Laomedon for the two magic horses which
he had won.

Laomedon, however, had never been known to keep
his word; and this time he did not depart from his usual
habits. He sent two horses, it is true, but instead of those
which Zeus had given to King Tros in return for Ganymede,
which were magic horses who could run like the wind

over the sea or the standing corn, he sent two chargers of ordinary, mortal breed.

Heracles vowed vengeance against Laomedon; but it was only when he came to settle at Trachis that he was able to set about gathering followers for this expedition of his own.

Leaving his young wife Deianira safely at Trachis, Heracles set out, accompanied by his nephew Iolaus, to seek for companions; and he turned first of all to his old friends Telamon and Peleus who had been his companions on his expedition against the Amazons, as well as during the Quest of the Golden Fleece and at the Calydonian Boar hunt.

Telamon lived at Salamis near Athens, and had married not long before. While Heracles was his guest a baby son was born to Telamon's queen, and was named Ajax.

Telamon and Peleus sat feasting with their guest when the baby boy was brought in for his father to see, and Heracles cried:

'By the will of Zeus this son of yours shall be a strong and mighty hero. See, I wrap about him the skin of the Lion, the first of my many Labours: may Ajax prove as bold as a lion and as strong and fearless!'

When the rejoicings were ended, Telamon gathered a fleet of six ships, and with Heracles in command they set sail for Troy. Now with Heracles were Telamon himself,

Peleus, Oicles, Iolaus and Deimachus, each in command of a ship.

They sailed quickly across the Aegean Sea and came unexpectedly to the land of Troy, where they anchored the ships, and leaving Oicles and his company to guard them, marched for the city itself.

King Laomedon was not prepared for this sudden invasion, but he armed as many men as he could, and made a forced march by secret ways to the place where the ships were moored.

He took old Oicles by surprise, and in the desperate battle which followed, Oicles was killed, and his men only saved the ships by entering them and putting out to sea.

Well pleased with this beginning, Laomedon marched back to Troy by his secret route, and after a brisk fight with some of Heracles's men, got into the city and barred the gates.

Heracles surrounded Troy and settled down to besiege it. But on this occasion the siege did not last long, for the walls, although built by the Immortals Poseidon and Apollo, were not themselves immortal since they had been helped in their work by a mortal, Aeacus, the father of Peleus and Telamon.

The first breach in the wall was made by Telamon, who knew from his father where the weakest place was to be found; and through the gap he rushed with his followers, while Heracles was still trying to storm the citadel. Very soon Heracles was in also, and the battle raged fiercely until King Laomedon lay dead, shot by the deadly arrows, and by him all his sons except the youngest. His name was Podarces, and he was spared because he had tried to persuade Laomedon to behave honestly and give up the magic horses.

When the walls were levelled with the ground, Heracles summoned before him all the captives. Among them was the Princess Hesione whom he had rescued from the sea monster, and who should have become his wife.

'But I am married already,' said Heracles, 'and so I will give this princess to my friend King Telamon; and in memory of what might have been, I will give her a bride-gift. Princess Hesione, you may choose one of these captives to go free.'

Then Hesione, weeping for the death of her father and brothers, knelt before Heracles and said:

'Great Hero of Greece, spare my brother Podarces and let him go free to rebuild Troy and reign there over my father's people.'

Heracles replied: 'Podarces has been spared, but he is my slave, the spoil of war. Yet I will grant your request, but you must buy him from me: you must pay something in ransom, if it be no more than your veil!'

Then Hesione plucked the veil from her head and with it bought the freedom of Podarces; and ever afterwards his name was changed to Priam, which means 'ransomed'.

When Heracles and his followers had sailed away, Priam gathered all the Trojans together and built the new city of Troy, a great, strong place with mighty walls and gates. And he married a wife called Hecuba, and they had many sons, the most famous of whom were Hector and Paris.

Meanwhile as Heracles and his little fleet of ships were sailing back towards Greece, his old enemy Hera could contain her hatred no longer. She knew that the Giants were stirring in their caves in the wild north and might make war on the Immortals at any moment; and she knew as well as Zeus himself that only with the help of Heracles could they be conquered, yet in her jealousy she made one last effort to destroy the son of Alcmena.

She called to her Hypnos, the spirit of Sleep, own brother to Death, and child of Night:

'Sleep, master of mortals and Immortals,' said Hera, 'go swiftly now to the couch of great Zeus, and lull his shining eyes to rest – for he has great need of you!'

Hypnos went to where Zeus lay, and spread his gentle wings over him, so that presently the great King of the Immortals slumbered peacefully.

Hera thereupon let loose the storm-winds from the north, and a great tempest descended upon the sea, and drove the ships before it, scudding over the waves and among the rocky islands, in deadly peril every moment.

Then indeed Heracles might have met his fate if Zeus had not awoken in time. When he saw what had happened, his wrath was very terrible. He took Hera and hung her by the wrists from heaven, with an iron anvil hanging from each foot; and when Hephaestus tried to set her free, Zeus took him by the leg and flung him out of Olympus, down on to the island of Lemnos, where he was found by the sea-nymph Thetis.

He ordered the storm-winds back to the island where Aeolus kept them in a cave until they were needed, and a great calm fell upon the Aegean Sea, just in time to save Heracles from being wrecked upon the rocky island of Cos.

But scarcely had Heracles and his companions landed, tired and exhausted, when King Eurypylus who ruled the island attacked him with a large force: for Hera had already sent him word that a band of pirates were about to land on the island.

The weary Greeks were defeated and scattered in the darkness, including Heracles himself. He was hotly pursued, since Eurypylus was particularly anxious to kill the captain of the pirates, and only escaped by hiding in a cottage. Here lived a large, fat woman who fled away into the darkness when she saw Heracles; and he had just time to dress himself in her clothes and bend over the cradle, when the men arrived at the door.

Seeing only the old woman, they went on towards the

centre of the island, and Heracles was able to rest and eat until his strength came back to him.

In the morning he gathered his scattered followers, attacked the Coans, and defeated them, killing King Eurypylus. They remained on the island of Cos for some time, refitting their ships before setting sail for Greece; and Heracles had been wounded in the battle.

Then one day the Immortal Queen of Wisdom and Strategy, Pallas Athena, came suddenly to Heracles:

'Up, most mighty of mortals!' she cried. 'The day has come for which you were born! For the Giants are loose upon the earth, and without the aid of the mortal Hero appointed, even the Immortals cannot withstand them!'

Then Athena took him up and carried him across the sea to the dread plain of fiery Phlegra, where the ground smokes and trembles like the crater of a volcano.

CHAPTER NINETEEN

THE BATTLE OF THE GIANTS

When on the smoky Phlegran field
　　Immortals fight the Giant clan,
Know that their lives shall only yield
　　To arrows of a mortal man;

And he, his Labours done, shall bide
　　For ever in Olympian ease;
And Hebe waits to be the bride
　　Of the Immortal, Heracles!

PINDAR
First Nemean Ode (Translated by R. L. G.)

19

The invasion so long dreaded and expected came suddenly. For Earth had made the Giants and hidden them away in great caves far to the north of Greece until the moment came when they were strong and fierce enough to assail heaven.

Then, as soon as Zeus seemed very much engaged in quarrelling with Hera and tossing Hephaestus out of heaven, the Giants came down into Greece and got ready to attack the Immortals.

They camped on the volcanic plain of Phlegra, and the first thing they did was to capture the golden-horned cattle of the Sun-Titan, Helios, and carry them off for food.

The leader of the Giants was called Alcyoneus, and he was immortal so long as he stayed in the land of Phlegra. And at first they attacked Olympus, hurling huge rocks and burning oak-trees.

'We cannot slay the Giants unaided!' cried Zeus. 'So much the Titan Prometheus told me. A mortal must kill them, when we have overcome them – the greatest Hero in all Greece, if he be brave and strong enough. And that man is Heracles! For this he was born, my son, and the son of a mortal woman. For this he has been trained all these years, and has accomplished such labours as no mortal did before, nor shall do again!'

Then he sent Athena to fetch Heracles. But meanwhile the words of Zeus had reached Earth, and she, fearing lest all her plots should come to nought, bade the Giants seek for a magic herb which would render them proof even against the mortal Hero.

Zeus learnt of this, and knowing that there was only a single plant of the magic herb, he instructed Athena to help Heracles in his search for it; and to prevent the Giants from finding it first, he ordered Helios to keep the Sun-chariot at home, and Selene the Moon-chariot also, that there might be no light on the earth save the feeble glimmer of the stars.

In this strange, unnatural twilight Heracles found the

herb; and when the sun rose again the great battle began.

Earth sent out a breath of fire from the subterranean caves of Phlegra, and the Giant King spoke in a terrible voice, crying:

'Giants, now is the hour! Tear up the mountains and hurl them at Olympus! Tear down the Immortals from their high thrones and bind them with our kinsmen the Titans in Tartarus! And one of you shall have Aphrodite to be his wife, and another shall have Artemis – while I, your king, claim Hera as my prize!'

The rocks hurtled through the air, and whole hilltops were torn away in the struggle.

And first of all, by Athena's direction, Heracles shot Alcyoneus with a poisoned arrow. But as soon as he fell to the ground he began to recover.

'Quick!' cried Athena. 'He cannot die so long as he remains in Phlegra! Drag him away into another country!'

So Heracles hoisted the still-breathing Giant on to his back and staggered with him over the border. There he flung him down and finished him with repeated blows of his club.

Returning to the battle, Heracles found that the Giant Porphyrion had assumed the lead and tried to carry off Hera. They had now piled up great rocks, and were fighting on the slopes of Olympus. Eros, the Lord of Love, wounded this Giant with his arrow, but the only result was to make him fall most desperately in love with Hera. This, at least, drew him from the battle, and when he saw his chance, Zeus felled him with a thunderbolt; and Heracles, returning just in time, settled him with an arrow.

The battle grew fast and furious now, and Heracles stood by to send in the shaft of death whenever an Immortal had laid a Giant low. When, for example, Apollo had smitten one in the eye with his bright shaft, or Hecate had burnt another with her torches; when Hephaestus had laid low a Giant with missiles of red-hot metal, or Dionysus brought down an enemy with his magic thysus, or Ares the War Lord smote home with his terrible spear.

Finally the remnants of the Giants fled in terror towards the south of Greece, all except the two greatest ones, Ephialtes and Otus. These made a last, desperate assault; and first of all they captured Ares himself and shut him up in a brass jar.

Then they piled Mount Ossa on top of Mount Pelion, and started climbing up towards Heaven, Ephialtes vowing that Hera should be his prize, and Otus that he would marry the Maiden Artemis.

In this emergency even Heracles was powerless to help, for these two Giants could only be killed by their own kind – neither man nor Immortal could do anything against them.

They were easily tricked, however, being as stupid as

Giants usually are; and when Zeus sent a message that he would give up Artemis to the most deserving of the two, they began to quarrel violently. While they were arguing Artemis turned herself into a white doe and ran suddenly between them. Each, eager to prove that *he* was at least the better marksman, hurled a spear at it. Both missed their mark, but each spear pierced the other Giant to the heart. Thus each was struck by his own kind, and so they died, and were chained to a pillar in Tartarus with fetters made of living vipers.

Meanwhile the other Giants fled, pursued closely by the Immortals and Heracles. One was caught by Poseidon, who broke off a piece of the island of Cos and buried him under it, making the Rock of Nisyros which still sticks up out of the sea near by.

The rest came to Arcadia, and at a place called Bathos the Immortals surrounded them and the final battle took place. There Hermes, wearing the Helmet of Invisibility which he had borrowed from Hades, struck down a Giant; and Ares, whom Hermes had just rescued from the brazen pot, wielded his spear to good effect, while Artemis sped home her arrows and Zeus whirled down his thunderbolts upon the doomed race of Giants. And Heracles, with his fatal shafts and his mighty club, made certain that there could be no recovery from the blows of the Immortals.

The last Giant left alive was Enceladus. Heracles had wounded him and when he saw all his companions, whom he had thought immortal, lying dead around him, he fled before the sword of the drunken Satyr, Silenus, who had accompanied Dionysus into the battle.

He rushed across Greece, waded the Adriatic Sea, and was at last overtaken by Athena at Cumae in Italy – where he still lies, breathing fire, under the volcano of Vesuvius. But some Roman writers believed that it was Enceladus, and not Typhon the Terrible, who lay imprisoned under Mount Etna in Sicily.

The battle was ended, the Giants destroyed and the Immortals were saved. Heracles, the great Hero, had done his work on earth, and Zeus was preparing to raise him to Olympus and make him an Immortal.

But, a mortal still and a very weary one at that, Heracles went to visit his friend Nestor at Pylos to rest after the battle. This was the same Nestor whom he had known on the *Argo* and at the Calydonian Boar hunt; and earlier still, he had fought against Nestor's father in a battle where both Hera and Hades tried in vain to overcome him and, though Immortals, both felt the sting of his arrows. After that battle, Heracles had set Nestor on the throne, and he found the young king always a staunch friend and ally.

Now at Pylos Heracles met his friend Tyndareus, father of Castor and Polydeuces, the rightful king of Sparta, who had been driven out by his wicked brother. Heracles already had a grievance against the usurper, who had killed a friend of his for merely striking a Spartan dog which attacked him. As soon therefore as Heracles was recovered from his weariness, he led an army to invade Sparta.

The army came mostly from Tegea, whose king feared to leave his little city unguarded, and would only march out with his men after Athena had given a lock of the Gorgon's hair to Heracles. This was concealed in a bronze jar and entrusted to the Princess Sterope: when, just as the king had expected, a troop of Spartans appeared suddenly in front of Tegea, she waved the lock of hair three times from the city wall – and the Spartans were seized with panic and fled back to Sparta.

There Heracles had already captured the city and killed the wicked king, with all his sons, and Tyndareus succeeded to the throne.

Heracles then set out for his home in Trachis, where Deianira was waiting eagerly for him. Not far from Trachis, on a headland overlooking the sea, he paused to raise an altar and offer a sacrifice to Zeus; and he sent his herald, Lichas, to Trachis for the robe which he usually wore on such occasions.

Now Deianira was intensely jealous, and from some chance remark made by Lichas she jumped to the conclusion that Heracles had grown tired of her and was bringing back a new wife called Iole. In actual fact this captive princess was destined to be the bride of their son, Hyllus.

Suddenly, Deianira remembered the love-charm which the dying Centaur, Nessus, had given her, and now she determined to use it. So she unsealed the jar, and quickly soaked the robe in it before sending it to Heracles in a casket. Then she tossed a bit of rag which had fallen into the jar out into the courtyard to dry.

Presently, as she sat happily weaving by her window, she glanced out and a sudden chill of terror struck her heart. For the piece of rag was twisting and burning in the sunlight till it turned into fine white powder like saw-dust; and under it were seething clots of foam like dark bubbles in fomenting wine.

In a panic Deianira jumped to her feet, screaming for Hyllus, and when he came she told him what had happened and begged him to go as swiftly as he could to where his father was performing the sacrifice.

Off went Hyllus in his fastest chariot: but when he reached the place, he realized that he was too late. Heracles had put on the robe; and as soon as the sun melted the Hydra's poison in the blood of Nessus with which the robe was anointed, it spread all over him and began to burn like liquid fire.

In vain Heracles tried to tear off the robe; when he did, it was only to tear the very flesh from his bones with it, while his blood hissed and bubbled like water when a red-hot iron is dropped into it.

Yelling with pain, Heracles flung himself into the

nearest stream: but the poison burned ever more fiercely, and that stream has been hot ever since, and is still called 'Thermopylae', or the 'hot ways'. Out of the boiling water sprang Heracles, mad with pain, and catching the unfortunate herald Lichas, who had brought him the robe, he swung him round his head and hurled him far out to sea. Then he went rushing through the woods, tearing boughs off the trees, until he came to Mount Oeta; where his strength forsook him and he sank to the ground.

Here Hyllus found him, and told him what had caused his terrible plight.

'I thought that Deianira had done this to slay me!' groaned Heracles. 'If she had, I would have killed her before I died.'

'She is dead already,' said Hyllus sadly. 'When she knew what she had done, she stabbed herself. But you may rest assured that she never dreamt the blood of Nessus was anything but a charm to retain your love.'

'Then my death is upon me,' said Heracles, 'for Athena warned me that the dead should slay me, though no living creature could. Now swear to do what I bid you: swear by the head of Zeus.'

Hyllus swore this most solemn of oaths, and then Heracles bade him heap a mighty pyre of wood on the mountain top. When this was done, Heracles dragged his tortured body on to it, lay down upon the skin of the Lion, with the Club under his head, and spoke to Hyllus:

'All is finished,' he said, 'and in a little while I shall be with the Immortals, as Zeus, my father, promised. Go now, wed Iole, and live happily. But first, set a light to this pyre!'

But Hyllus drew away, weeping sorely, and no one dared obey the dying Hero. At last Heracles saw a young man driving a flock of sheep, and called to him:

'Young man, come here and I will give you a great reward if you do what I command you!'

The youth came and stood beside the pyre, and when he saw who lay upon it, he began to tremble and said:

'My lord Heracles, I know you well: for my father Poeas the Argonaut has often spoken of you, and of how he alone of mortals once held your bow and loosed an arrow from it, to lay low Talos the Brass Man of Crete.'

'Then, by the friendship that was between your father and me,' gasped Heracles, 'I charge you to set a light to this pyre. Take my bow and arrows as your reward – for you must be Philoctetes, the only son of Poeas. Take them, and remember that without those arrows the city of Troy can never fall to mortal invaders.'

Weeping as he did so, Philoctetes took the bow and arrows. Then he kindled fire and set a light to the great heap of wood. Then he drew back, while the flames roared upwards.

Suddenly there was a loud peal of thunder, and a cloud seemed to pass across the pyre, putting out the flames.

And when Philoctetes drew near to the blackened wood, there was no trace of Heracles.

But on Olympus, with his earthly, mortal part burned away, Zeus was welcoming Heracles – henceforth an Immortal. And now at last Hera forgot her jealousy and made him welcome also; and to show that she too honoured the Hero who had saved the Immortals, she gave him her daughter Hebe to be his wife in Olympus.

Meanwhile, on earth, Alcmena died of grief when she heard that her son Heracles was dead: and her grandsons put her body in a coffin to carry her to her grave. But by command of Zeus the cunning Immortal thief, Hermes, stole away the body and put a stone in its place: and so Alcmena was brought to live in the happy islands of the Elysian Fields.

But the sons of Heracles, thinking that the coffin was remarkably heavy, opened it and discovered what had happened. So they set up the stone near Thebes as a monument to Alcmena: but, like Heracles himself, she had no grave anywhere on earth.

Epilogue

Although the Age of the Heroes did not end with the death of Heracles, the end was drawing very near, and almost all the tales of the Heroes were told – except for one.

That strange time of myth and legend – of history which was more than half a fairy tale and fairy tales that might have been true – ended in the greatest adventure of all, one of the world's most famous romances, 'the Tale of Troy divine'.

Already some of its heroes were born and growing up: Philoctetes, who lit the pyre for Heracles, was one of them, and the sons of the Argonauts, of Peleus and Laertes, of Heracles himself, were to play their parts and win immortal fame before Troy.

But that story is a whole book in itself, and is told in *The Tale of Troy*, another volume in the Puffin series.

AUTHOR'S NOTE

The stories of the ancient Greek myths and legends have been told and re-told times without number and in every way, from short poems to long novels. And the adventures of the Heroes may be found in simple form in numberless volumes, the most famous of which are perhaps Charles Kingsley's *The Heroes* and Nathaniel Hawthorne's *Tanglewood Tales*.

In the present book I have, however, tried to present the old tales in a new way. My predecessors have taken isolated stories and re-told them at various lengths – but they have, as a rule, remained isolated. Here I have tried to tell the tale of the Heroic Age as that single whole which the Greeks believed it to be.

The result, which takes the story from the myths of the making of the universe down to the death of Heracles, has been to gather into a sequence some of the world's most famous stories. As this is not a mere outline of Greek Mythology, however, the stories, as they weave in and out of one another, have grown or shrunk in importance.

Thus the great tales such as those of Perseus, Theseus, or the Argonauts have demanded whole chapters to themselves, while brief adventures, however famous, such as those of Orpheus and Eurydice, or King Midas, become incidents or 'inset' stories. I do not think, however, that many of the well-known tales have been omitted, except for the misfortunes of Oedipus and the subsequent expeditions against Thebes; and a few of the 'metamorphosis' legends such as those of Narcissus or Hyacinthus – which are really items in a Classical Dictionary, even though some re-tellers who use Ovid as their main source spin them out into separate tales.

One story, and that the most famous of all, is missing – the Tale of Troy. But that, being a subject of such size and importance, it has seemed best to tell separately, and it is to be found in *The Tale of Troy*. The story of the Heroic Age divides naturally at the death of Heracles; all the tales of later heroes form part of the great saga of Helen of Sparta, of the siege and fall of Troy, and of the wanderings and returns of Odysseus and the other Heroes – and that demands a volume to itself.

A detailed list of the sources which I have used for this book would be out of place – a vast list of authors and reference numbers ranging backwards and forwards throughout the two thousand years of Greek literature which separate Homer from Eustathius. Sometimes the dialogue is modelled on the original Greek, and sometimes it is my own: but I have, to the best of my ability, used my multitudinous sources honestly. I have selected, but I hope that I have never falsified my originals; I may have assumed dialogue, but I have added no single incident, so far as I am aware, nor made any alteration in a legend, though I have sometimes omitted where desirable.

There are two small exceptions to this rule. The first is the suppression of the name of the 'witch-wife' who tried to poison Theseus when he came to Athens: if she were Medea, Theseus could hardly have been an Argonaut! The other is that I have followed Kingsley in allowing an old servant, the only man who ever fitted the Bed of Procrustes exactly, to warn Theseus: Kingsley *may* have had an authority for this, but I have not been able to trace it.

Otherwise I have full Classical authority for everything in this book. Indeed, though I have sometimes used a Latin author for details or descriptions, I can say that I have ancient *Greek* authority for everything except the adventure with Cacus.

Finally, it is hardly necessary to do more than remark on my use throughout of the correct Greek names for the gods of Ancient Greece. The habit of using their Latin equivalents has been broken completely during the last hundred years, though it lingers still in reprints of Hawthorne. In deference to general literary tradition, however, I have used the Latinized spellings – Phoebus Apollo for Phoibos Apollon, Eurydice for Eurydike – and so on. I have added a list of the Latin versions of the names of the gods and goddesses lest any reader should be puzzled by meeting them in this alien disguise.

But indeed the gods and heroes of Ancient Greece can never seem as aliens to us. Their stories are a part of the world's heritage, they are part of the background of our literature, our speech, of our very thoughts. We cannot come to them too early, nor are we ever likely to outgrow them as we pass from such simple re-tellings as this to the Greek authors themselves – at first in the English versions of Lang or Murray or Rieu, and then, if we are lucky, to the lovely echoing phrases of the Greek itself. Once found, the magic web of old Greek myth and legend is ours by right – and ours for life. Through good or ill –

Old shapes of song that do not die
Shall haunt the halls of memory.

ROGER LANCELYN GREEN

THE GODS AND GODDESSES OF ANCIENT GREECE

Greek	*Latin*
CRONOS	SATURN
RHEA	CYBELE
HELIOS	SOL (The Sun)
EOS	AURORA (The Dawn)
SELENE	LUNA (The Moon)
ZEUS	JUPITER OR JOVE
POSEIDON	NEPTUNE
HADES	PLUTO OR DIS
DEMETER	CERES
HESTIA	VESTA
HERA	JUNO
PERSEPHONE	PROSERPINE
ARES	MARS
DIONYSUS	BACCHUS
HERMES	MERCURY
HEPHAESTUS	VULCAN
ATHENA	MINERVA

ARTEMIS	DIANA
APHRODITE	VENUS
ASCLEPIUS	AESCULAPIUS
HERACLES	HERCULES OR ALCIDES

APOLLO, PAN, and HECATE are the same in both.

PUFFIN CLASSICS

Tales of the Greek Heroes

With Puffin Classics, the adventure isn't
over when you reach the final page.
Want to discover more about your favourite
characters, their creators and their worlds?
Read on . . .

CONTENTS

Name: Roger Lancelyn Green
Born: 2 November 1918 in Norwich, England
Died: 8 October 1987 in Poulton, Cheshire
Nationality: English
Lived: in Oxford and his family home in Cheshire, which the
Greens had owned for over 900 years
Married: to June Green
Children: three children: Scirard, Richard and Priscilla

What was he like?

Roger was a man who loved storytelling and was fascinated by
traditional fairy tales, myths and legends from around the world.

Where did he grow up?

He was born in Norwich and went to boarding school in Surrey.
Roger was often ill, though, and couldn't go to school – so he
spent lots of time at the family's manor house in the county of
Cheshire. His family had been wealthy, and there was a huge
library in their house. He spent many hours reading the old
books there, and this is probably where his love of myths and
legends started.

What did he do apart from writing books?

In the course of his life Roger was a professional actor, a
librarian and a teacher. He was also a member of the Inklings
Club in Oxford, a group of friends who read, and commented
on, each other's work. Its members included C. S. Lewis

(author of *The Chronicles of Narnia*) and J. R. R. Tolkien (author of *The Lord of the Rings* and *The Hobbit*).

If it hadn't been for Roger, *The Chronicles of Narnia* might never have been published. In 1949 Roger went to dinner with C. S. Lewis. Lewis read Roger two chapters of *The Lion, the Witch and the Wardrobe*. He also informed Roger that he'd read them to Tolkien a few weeks before, who had told Lewis that he didn't think they were very good. Roger disagreed. He thought they were great, and he encouraged Lewis to get them published. Roger even thought of the series title, *The Chronicles of Narnia*, and he went on to become the very first reader of all of the rest of the Narnia stories.

Where did Roger get the idea for Tales of the Greek Heroes?
Roger had always loved reading adventure stories and fairy tales, but when he went on a cruise in 1937 he discovered a passion for Greece too. He was fascinated by the country, its myths and its legends, and went on to retell the ancient stories in his own lively, vivid way.

What did people think of Tales of the Greek Heroes when it was first published in 1953?
Roger's *Tales of the Greek Heroes* was a bestseller during the 1950s and 1960s and has been in print ever since.

What other books did he write?
Retellings of the Egyptian, Greek and Norse myths, plus retellings of the legends of Robin Hood and King Arthur. He also wrote many books for adults, including a biography of his friend C. S. Lewis.

The Romans knew the Greek gods and goddesses by different names. For example, Zeus was known as Jupiter, Aphrodite was Venus and the Romans knew Heracles as Hercules. See pages 271–2 for a full list.

The first Olympic Games were held in honour of the Greek King of the Gods, Zeus. They took place in Olympia, which was named after Mount Olympus, the highest mountain on mainland Greece and, according to Greek mythology, the home of the greatest gods and goddesses.

Roger Lancelyn Green tells of how the Minotaur – a fearsome creature with a great human body and the head and neck of a bull – roamed a labyrinth beneath the Palace of Cnossos. Did you know that the palace ruins in Crete are now visited by one million tourists every year?

Greek myths and legends have inspired many well-known films. Here are just three of the most popular:

Jason and the Argonauts (1963)
This film tells the tale of how Jason and his band of Argonauts battle the Harpies, Talos and the Hydra to win the Golden Fleece. It stars Todd Armstrong as Jason.

Clash of the Titans (1981)
Starring Sir Laurence Olivier as mighty Zeus, Claire Bloom as Hera, Dame Maggie Smith as Thetis and Ursula Andress as Aphrodite, this film was a box-office hit.

Troy (2004)
The star-studded cast of this multimillion-dollar epic included Brad Pitt, Orlando Bloom and Eric Bana. The film retold the Greek myth of Helen, a woman so beautiful that she caused a war between Troy and Sparta.

IMMORTALS

Cronos – the father of the gods Zeus, Hades and Poseidon and the goddesses Hera, Hestia and Demeter.

Rhea – Cronos's wife and the mother of gods and goddesses.

Helios – the god who drove the chariot of the sun across the sky each day.

Eos – the Goddess of the Dawn.

Selene – the Goddess of the Moon.

Zeus – the King of the Gods.

Poseidon – the God of the Sea.

Hades – the God of the Underworld.

Demeter – the Goddess of Grain and Fertility.

Hestia – the Goddess of Home and Family.

Hera – the Goddess of Women and Marriage.

Persephone – the Goddess of the Underworld.

Ares – the God of Warfare.

Dionysus – the God of Wine.

Hermes – messenger of the Gods.

Hephaestus – the God of Fire and Technology.

Athena – the Goddess of Heroic Endeavour.

Artemis – the Goddess of Forests, Hills and Fertility.

Aphrodite – the Goddess of Love.

Asclepius – the God of Medicine.

Heracles – the greatest of the Greek heroes.

Apollo – the God of Light, the Sun, Truth and Prophecy, among many other things.

Pan – the God of Shepherds and their flocks.

Hecate – the Goddess of Wilderness and Childbirth.

MORTALS

Prometheus – the Titan who stole fire from Zeus and gave it to the Mortals.

Typhon – the last of the Titans and the biggest, most terrible creature ever known on the Earth.

Perseus – the hero who killed Medusa.

Admetus – a young, brave, handsome prince who was kind to Apollo.

Theseus – son of Aegeus, King of Athens, he was strong, brave and wise.

Jason – son of the rightful King of Iolcus.

Argonauts – a group of heroes led by Jason on a quest for the Golden Fleece.

Meleager – one of the Argonauts.

Atalanta – a skilful and courageous princess.

CREATURES AND MONSTERS

Titans – a family of giants. The last of the Titans was Typhon, a terrible creature with one hundred heads.

Gorgons – female monsters, the most terrible being Medusa, who had writhing snakes instead of hair.

Cyclopes – giants with only one eye in the middle of the forehead.

Satyrs – wild wood-dwellers with pointed ears and little horns.

Nymphs – female creatures who were linked with places such as rivers, mountains and seas.

Centaurs – creatures that had the upper body of a human and the lower body of a horse.

Harpies – terrible, winged women with great claws.

Why do you think the Greek myths and legends were first told?

Many phrases used in everyday speech come from Greek mythology. In this book, Roger Lancelyn Green tells us how everything that King Midas touched turned to gold. What do you think it means nowadays if someone is said to have the 'Midas touch'?

Today, people still refer to 'a Herculean task' or say that someone has 'Herculean strength'. What does 'Herculean' have to do with Greek mythology?

Roger Lancelyn Green weaves many of the Greek myths and legends together to form one long, unbroken story that helps to put all of the tales in context. Do you like this way of telling the tales of the Greek heroes or would you rather read lots of separate stories?

If you were a character in Greek mythology, would you prefer to be a Mortal or an Immortal? Why?

The Twelve Labours of Heracles are a series of tasks that he must complete in order to be forgiven for the terrible things he has done. Can you think of a brand-new thirteenth Labour for Heracles to perform? Don't forget, it should be impossibly difficult and *very* dangerous!

Typhon is one of the most terrible creatures in Greek mythology. The illustrator Alan Langford has drawn him (see page 59), but why not create your own version, based on the description below?

He was so tall that as he walked far out in the sea the waves came only a little way above his knees; and when he stood upon the dry land, the stars became entangled in his hair. He was terrible to look at, for from his shoulders grew a hundred heads, with dark, flickering serpent tongues and flaming eyes . . . From this monster's shoulders grew dragons' wings; and his hands were so strong that he could lift mountains with them.

Look up the place names that the author mentions in an atlas. You could look for Sicily, Crete and Delphi, and there are many more in this book. (But watch out – some of the spellings may be a little different from those used by Roger Lancelyn Green. For example, 'Cos' is often spelled 'Kos'.) If you're ever lucky enough to go to Greece, you could visit them for yourself.

Some myths explain natural phenomena, such as why Mount Etna erupts (see page 66). Why not make up your own myth to describe an unusual or everyday event?

If you've enjoyed reading any of the excerpts by other authors and poets that precede each chapter, why not look up the original and read the whole thing?

bier – a stand on which a corpse or coffin is placed

castanets – small, curved pieces of wood or ivory joined in pairs and clicked rhythmically to accompany dancing

destiny – the events that will happen to a person in the future, regarded as predetermined by fate

faggot – a bundle of sticks

fetters – chains or shackles used to keep someone prisoner

impious – wicked

isthmus – a thin strip of land that links two larger pieces of land

kine – cows

lea – an open area of grassy land or farm land

oracle – someone who is considered to be very wise or who is able to predict the future

osier – a small willow tree

pan-pipes – a musical instrument made of pipes of different lengths joined together; it is played by blowing across the ends of the pipes

plough-share – the main cutting blade of a plough

pretender – a person who claims that a title or position is rightfully theirs

prophecy – a prediction

sacrifice – when an animal or person is killed in honour of a god

scythe or sickle – a tool with a long, curved blade used for cutting crops

servitude – slavery

sinew – tough, stringy tissue that connects muscle to bone

smote – past tense of the verb 'to smite', meaning to strike

strife – conflict

syrinx – a set of pan-pipes

woo – to try to win a woman's heart

yore – long ago